Thank you to my 1  a non-domestic mother and wife for the past year.

To Carla, Gloria, Mike and Jan, who always said I could do it, love you all.

To all my friends and family who have supported me throughout, hugs.

To my new friends
Ish & Josie

Melody Adams
2017

Preface

The electromagnetic pulse, that burned out just about everything electric or that had digital circuits on the planet, had been predicted by Doom-Sayers and scientists alike. The solar flare took out every electronic device that hadn't been protected. Many anti-government type survivalists were good to go, having planned on EMP's from terrorist attacks or a Big Brother action from the government. These people had long ago installed Faraday cages, or EMP proof boxes around their generators, HAM radios, computers and every day electric devices that made life much easier to live. Much of the world population had been too caught up in their own day-to-day miseries to pay any attention though. Governments had scrambled up to the last minute of the event, but Canada and the United States were the only two countries that came even close to being ready, and sadly not nearly enough. Most of the other countries of the world were taken back to Stone Age technology.

The first few minutes after the EMP had been a vision of hell on earth as jets and planes fell from the sky to explode in fiery balls rising back up to the heavens. Trains lost power and their conductors could not control the cars as they flew past curves out into space before crashing like dominos one after another. Cars and trucks formed huge pileups on busy city freeways. People panicked, tempers exploded and riots killed many more before the day was done.

Heart attacks were common, as were asthma attacks. Hospitals lost so many of the ill or wounded that the morgues filled too quickly. Within a month, mass burnings of the dead were a common sight, due to the fact that mass graves could not be dug. All the bulldozers and heavy equipment sat where they too had died.

Criminals began to run in amok in the cities. Good people; families, senior citizens, neighborhoods tried to make it alone, found that it had been a foolish mistake when looters or gangs broke through flimsy wooden doors to pillage all that had been stocked in pantries and basements. Some survived these attacks to try and find more food and shelter elsewhere. Others were not so fortunate. Violence fed violence. Blood ran in the streets as a new world began to form from the remnants of the old one.

The military pronounced martial law in many of the major cities. Sadly, in some cities, this just replaced the gang violence with a different uniform. Depending on the commander in each metro area, some cities became more prison than sanctuary.

The human race, though, could not be brought down; it hung on with the same tenacity that had pulled it up from caves a millennium ago.

Chapter one

"Kevin, you know how to make a girl feel good! Kicking your butt just puts a smile on my face!" Rusty brushed the dust from her jeans and backed up from her brother, laughing.

"Yeah well... just bite me Rusty!" Kevin yelped when Rusty rushed forward to do exactly what he suggested.

As he ran into the sporting goods store to escape his sister's teeth, Rusty, still laughing, strolled down the empty street towards Fred's Foods.

She studied her own reflection in the plate glass window of the lifeless grocery store.

Born Beatrice Morgan Callahan, she had been dubbed "Rusty" when her grandfather had commented during his first visit to see her that her cry sounded like a rusty screen door being opened. The nickname had stuck.

Now, looking at the woman facing her in a bulky olive drab jacket and three shirts hid her willowy frame. The torn and tattered jeans over the steel toed black boots showed off her long legs though. She had never thought of herself as pretty. Sure, she did have a brilliant shade of blue coloring her eyes, but her mouth was too wide, her nose too sharp. At least in her opinion. Her thick, black hair was her favorite thing about herself. It was long, thick and shiny and currently pulled back in a ponytail, poked out of the Mt. Rushmore cap from her last vacation.

Last vacation ever. She thought sardonically. *Wonder what the chances are that I find a bottle of mascara in there? Just get in there and get back out so you can give Kevin another bottle of whoop ass.*

Smirking, she stepped into the store through the broken door, side stepping glass that was scattered all over the tile.

Chapter two

The store was eerily quiet except for the sound of small rodents scurrying away from her as she walked up and down the aisles, along with the broken glass and spilt food crunching under foot.

Rusty bent to scan under shelves, grimacing as cockroaches scattered. She stood and was doing a happy dance, holding the small bag of rice the disgusting little bugs had been trying to get into.

Suddenly the door to the back stockroom opened and two men stepped into the aisle Rusty was standing in, quietly speaking to each other.

All three froze in shock at actually seeing another occupant in the store. Rusty darted a look to the front, looking for Kevin and an easy escape route. No brother in sight.

Suddenly, she feinted right, towards the front of the store and then dashed left down the aisle. She took the first left that she came to and ran at a full tilt to the far end, hoping to make it to the main aisle before the pair of men. She reached it, relieved to see no one blocking her path. One more aisle and she would be out the door, but as she came up to the empty meat counter, the younger of the two men met her. Both stopped, gasping for breath.

The sound of glass crunching beneath a shoe had Rusty whirling. Behind her the older man had come up, panting for breath. He looked down at the bag that Rusty still grasped. He held out his hand as he continued to move slowly forward.

"Give me the bag girlie, and we'll leave you in peace." His raspy voice held the Ozark twang of the region and matched the hillbilly look of the old man in his torn overalls and worn down work boots, much like her own. His face wasn't thin and hollowed, but filled out and healthy looking beneath the brown and gray beard. Rusty even caught a whiff of bacon coming from the man.

She fought down her fear and gripped the small bag tightly. Joey Wilder, a ten year old boy back at the farm had recently had a bout of stomach problems. Just this morning she had heard Joey's father, Drew wish for some bland, white rice for his son.

"Sorry, Mister, but I need this worse than you two. You look pretty well fed, if I do say so. Here," She dug into her pocket as she spoke, "I'll give you..."

Whether the two saw her movement as threatening or they just wanted compliance, she didn't know. The old man rushed her. His hand grabbed the shoulder of her jacket and dragged her up against his body as his other hand reached for the bag of rice.

Instinct and daily training kicked in, as Rusty swiftly brought her knee up with as much force as she had, connecting with the old man's groin.

The man's eyes crossed as he fell to the ground with a strangled cry.

Rusty was turning to face the younger man as he slammed into her, taking her down to the ground. She saw his fist rise a second before all the breath went out of her lungs as he punched her in the stomach. She noticed that his eyes were different colors, one soft brown, and the other sky blue. There wasn't hate or anger in his eyes, as she would expect, but shock and then sadness.

Then all the air was sucked from her lungs and she couldn't seem to get it back. The rice was ripped from her hand as she lay gasping like a grounded fish and blackness edged her vision.

She heard the younger man struggle to get the old man up on his feet then stumble back to the storeroom, followed by sound of a door crashing against the building as they exited the store.

After a few moments Rusty was able to get her breath back and struggled to sit up. It was sore as hell where the man had slugged her, but she didn't bother to look under her old army jacket and multiple shirts. Looking wouldn't make it feel better. She finally picked herself up and stumbled to the front door. Reaching into her pocket, she was reassured to find the dried up apple still there. It wasn't much, but the seeds represented future food. She would have gladly given it to the strangers.

She stood in the middle of the street, still feeling off. She saw Kevin come out of the sporting goods store down the block. The truck still sat by the curb where he had parked it. As he opened the door to get in, he noticed her standing in the street and yelled happily about finding "stuff".

Unwilling to share her humiliating story with her brother, she flipped him off as he rolled up in the old 1949 Chevy truck that she should have been driving, and continued on down the road, headed for the house, even though it was five miles out of town. He laughingly begged her to get in the truck, as his shaggy black hair ruffled in the open window. She would have refused, but her head was pounding and her stomach felt heavy and uncomfortable. She finally climbed in and promptly fell asleep, ignoring her snickering younger sibling.

Chapter three

Dawson was guarding the gate when they rolled up, back at the house. The sign hanging from the gate read, "Fort Repose".

The retired Army colonel, doctor and unofficial leader of the group, Josh Martin had named the homestead after a small town in a post-apocalyptic novel, "Alas, Babylon" by Pat Frank.

Rusty woke, feeling worse from the short nap, to hear Kevin bragging about finding several packages of arrowheads and shafts along with some fishing line.

She stepped out of the truck. Kevin pulled away, headed to the back of the house to park the truck inside the barn. Stopping long enough by Dawson's side to tell him to be on the lookout for the two scruffy men, she turned to head up the path to the house, about fifty yards from the gate. She just wanted to lie down for a bit, before helping with supper, it was her week on kitchen rotation.

Dawson was a huge man, a former bouncer at a bar in Tulsa, Oklahoma. His tattoos and piercings belied the fact that he acted goofy over kittens and puppies. The gun on his hip and rifle on his shoulder though, proved he would protect what was now his home.

He had joined the group last spring after a freezing winter spent on the road.

Dawson had left Tulsa with a kid sister. They had traveled north east into Missouri, heading for a summer cabin their uncle had owned. Dawson had left the small house early one morning to try and hunt up some food.

While he was gone she had been killed by a gang of AWOL soldiers. He had thought getting her away from the city would save her. He had been devastated and set on revenge.

It was while on the trail of the renegades that Dawson came to New Springs. He had missed them in the small town of Citadel, just on the north side of New Springs. He had stayed long enough to bury the old man the soldiers savagely beaten. Before the old man died, in Dawson's arms, he had described the five soldiers.

Rounding the street corner onto Main Street in New Springs, Dawson spotted the group of men. They had surrounded two women. Luckily, only crude suggestions were being thrown around by the men at the point. The women had knives drawn and where back to back in fighting stances.

The five men had barely registered Dawson's presence at the abandoned gas station before he had broken one man's neck and shot two others. One of the two remaining ex-soldiers had gone for his gun on his hip, but not before the enraged blonde giant had slammed his head into the side of the building. After Dawson had finished with what was left of the man, he had turned to face the remaining soldier, only to find that the two woman where chasing him down the street with their knives. The man had been fast though and had managed to get away. So far, he hadn't been seen in the area, nor if he had an iota of smarts, would he return.

Dawson had been practically dragged back to the house by Susan and Kate, fed, put to bed and had woke up to his clean clothes waiting at the end of the cot, Josh sitting in a chair across the room and an invitation to remain in New Springs with Josh's group. Dawson had accepted and was now part of the growing family.

"Sure you're alright Rusty? You're not looking so hot. I can go get Josh, he's out with Griff checkin' the horses in the south pasture." Dawson's concern was evident.

Rusty turned, slightly concerned herself when the world continued to turn when she stopped. She was suddenly just so tired. "Thanks Daws, but I'm okay. Just need to close my eyes for a while. I'll see ya at supper tonight."

Rusty managed to stumble through the large rambling house, without notice from any other inhabitants. She heard Susan in the kitchen, scolding one of the children for not washing their hands after leaving eating a cookie. Most everyone else was outside in the fields weeding or picking vegetables from the crops or sleeping, preparing for tonight's guard duty.

Out of breath from the three flights of stairs to the room, she staggered into the small apartment and shut the door. Her last thought was that maybe something was wrong with her as the room grew dim around her, and she fell unconscious

Chapter four

The trestle table in the large kitchen was nearly full, and it would fit twelve easily. Two chairs on both ends and two long benches were all filled with people of all shapes and sizes, young and old. Two young women, an older man with a black patch over his left eye and a young boy of ten were scurrying between the counters, stove and the table piling food along its length.

Josh Martin, called "Doc Martin" by most of the young people of the group, retained his military-style crew cut, leaving little of the silver hair on his head. At fifty five years old he remained in perfect shape due to his daily workouts, in every season, regardless of weather.

He was at the far end of the table talking with Kevin about the trip that he and Rusty had come back from earlier.

"Well, we were pretty sure that as small as New Springs is, most of the supplies would have been scavenged by now, hell, we scavenged most of it. I'm sure Colleen will be pleased with the arrows, not sure how we missed them to begin with."

Colleen was the most successful hunter in the clan and had grown up in the Ozarks hunting for her family's supper. She, her husband, Frank and their ten year old son, Thomas, had joined the group during the winter when Colleen brought an ailing Frank in to see Josh.

"I do wish you had taken Tobias or Drew with you, Dawson tells me that Rusty had a run in with a couple of men. What the hell were you thinking, splitting up to search for supplies? You know the protocol as well as any of us." He frowned at Rusty's younger brother who resembled her so much, it was obvious that they were siblings.

"Hell, I know Josh. It's just that Rusty can rile me up faster than a red hanky calls a bull. She wanted to drive and it was my turn. We had been arguing the whole trip in, seems stupid now when I think about it."

Kevin felt the red creep up his neck as he recalled Rusty kicking his ass in the middle of the street, just like she always did when it came down to a fight. Of course, he left that little piece of info out of his story. There seemed no need to share his humiliation.

"She didn't say anything to me about any men! She was still pissed, oh sorry Kate, she was still mad at me when she got in the truck. She wouldn't talk to me."

He hung his head as Kate growled "Potty mouth," as she leaned between him and Josh to replace the empty basket of rolls with another.

"All I'm saying is that you were lucky this time. If you and your sister can't work as a team, I can't have the two of you going out anymore, at least not together. Where is Rusty anyway? She's usually here or in the kitchen as soon as she smells food." He smiled as he spoke. Rusty's appetite was well known. For such a slip of a girl, she could challenge even the behemoth, Dawson, when it came to eating.

As Josh spoke, Griffin Thompson approached the table. Long, shaggy brown hair was constantly being pushed back out of his eyes by long, graceful fingers. Griffin was the tallest in the group, taller even than Dawson. He wasn't a skinny tall though, muscles filled out the plaid shirt and black jeans he wore. Working with pachyderms over the years and then living on the land had given him a grace more commonly seen on ancient Greek and Roman vases portraying the first Olympians.

Griffin was close to Rusty, they had survived the pulse's chaos together and managed to make it out of Kansas City alive, a rare thing in those days of panic, violence and blood.

Traveling together to pick up Kevin in a private military school in Kansas, Griffin and Rusty grew closer daily. They had worked together at the Kansas City Zoo before the EMP, and had been friends. Rusty had worked with the big cats and Griffin with the elephants. Both had degrees in Animal Science and had gone to the same school in Minnesota. They had only met though when Griffin had been hired at the Kansas City Zoo two years ago. Griffin was twenty nine to Rusty's twenty five, they had missed each other in Minnesota by one semester. Griffin had graduated and moved on to Florida while Rusty was just beginning school.

Griffin had no family to look for after the solar flare and following apocalypse and had decided that Rusty shouldn't go out into that newly violent world alone. As they traveled on into Kansas, they grew from coworkers into a couple. Now Griffin and Rusty made up two of the fifteen that was their group of survivors.

"She looked a little off when she and Kevin came back in, said she was just tired and was going to go rest before supper." Dawson paused from buttering a biscuit to suggest.

"I'll go take a look." Griffin turned away from the table and headed for the staircase in the hall.

The old house's staircase creaked and groaned as Griffin made his way up the two flights of steep, narrow stairs to what had been the servant quarters many years ago. The house had been on the National Registry for Historical Buildings before the Pulse. The bronze plaque claiming so was still attached to the wall outside by the front door. Thankfully, it had received good care from previous owners for those many years, providing a perfect sanctuary for the small band of survivors now.

Pausing only long enough to slowly open the bedroom door, Griffin entered their room. Rusty was in bed, as suggested. Griffin thought it odd that she was still in her jacket and boots. She was rolled up in a tight, little ball in the center of the bed. He slowly settled on the edge of the mattress and gently ran his hand through her black hair and down her relaxed cheek. Then he noticed that she wasn't relaxed at all, there was a crease between her eyebrows that she usually had when she was worried, working up to mad. As he became more aware of her whole body, he could feel the tension trembling through her.

"Rusty wake up, dinners ready." He gently shook her shoulder, in doing so he moved her hands that were wrapped around her abdomen. Her right arm slowly fell to the bed, he saw it was smeared with red in the dim lighting of fading day.

He quickly reached for a match near the old fashioned kerosene lamp on the small table by the bed. Striking the match, he quickly lit the wick of the lamp and turned the flame up as high as possible. Turning back to Rusty, he was shocked at the lack of coloring in her face. She was already fair skinned, but now she looked the shade of rice paper in the light.

Gently rolling her on to her back, he pulled back the old green army jacket that Rusty favored, to reveal a worn beige sweater that was sticky, wet with redness. Griffin's eyes widened as he slowly lifted the shirt to see blood slowly welling out of an inch long gash on her left side of her stomach.   Jumping up, Griffin rushed to the door and yelled down the stairs, "Josh, get up here! Rusty's hurt!"

Chapter five

More than a dozen feet could be heard rushing up the stairs even as Rusty moaned. Griffin stood as Josh burst into the room. "I think she's been stabbed."

Josh calmly came over, sat on the bed and did a quick examination of her. Lifting her lids he looked in her eyes, checked her pulse on her limp wrist and finally looked at the wound. Pressing on her stomach gently in several places, he finally turned to the gathering of people smashed in the room.

"Susan, I'm going to need the surgery prepped, scrub up, I'll need your assistance. Missy, we'll need as much hot water as you can heat up in the next hour. Tyrone, make sure all the lamps are filled in the surgery, with this fading light, I'll need them, everyone else out."

He issued orders just as he had in the Army twenty years ago and later in the emergency room in St. Luke's Hospital in Kansas City. His silver, gray hair was still cut military issue and he could make a hard-core Hell's Angel jump to attention when he barked an order.

In seconds the room was cleared except for Kevin, Griffin and Josh. Kevin had tears in his eyes; guilt was crowding out all other thoughts.

"Stabbed? Griff said she was stabbed. Oh, God. When she was in the freaking store by herself…" Kevin was overwhelmed with fear for his sister.

Josh calmly put his arm around Kevin's shoulders and turned him towards the door. "Kevin, I need you to stay calm and help Missy get the fire stoked up. We need that hot water fast. You know I'll do everything I can for your sister. She's strong and a fighter; that's in her favor."

Ushering Kevin from the room, and staying at the door until he was sure the young man was moving down the stairs, Josh turned to Griffin.

"Can you handle being here, or do I need to find a job for you too? I can't do my job if I'm worried you're going to faint or throw up on the floor at the first drop of blood, but I'm telling you now, I could use your help."

Griffin was still standing by the bed, looking at Rusty. He slowly turned to face the older man. His face had lost all its color, but he looked determined.

"I'm staying Josh. Rusty needs me; I won't walk out on her. Just tell me what you need me to do."

"All right, then I need you to help me carry her down to the surgery. Find out from Kevin or Dawson when they came back to the farm. She's been bleeding since the grocery store. I'm guessing it's not a bad bleeder or she'd have bled out by now. Her pulse is thready but not to the extreme."

He paused, sighing heavily, "God, what I would give for a sterile O.R."

Chapter six

A few hours later, Josh closed the incision with tiny stitches, sighed and stood back and stretched his arms high in the air feeling his spine lengthen and pop as kinks worked themselves out.

Speaking softly to Susan, who had worked by his side, "Go ahead and clean the incision and keep an eye on her vitals for a few hours. Let's not move her just yet. She was damn fortunate that the knife did as little damage as it did, but she still lost a significant amount of blood."

He removed the surgical gloves and mask and tossed them in the can below the table then turned to place a hand on Susan's shoulder, giving it a slight squeeze.

"I couldn't have done this without you Susan."

Doctor Josh Martin felt the dull flush creep up his neck. He hadn't felt the slightest nervousness about working side by side with Susan. Now that the life and death fight on the surgery table was over though his tongue turned to wood and refused to move, and he would swear later that his brain hit a black, hard wall when asked to form simple words of gratitude to the petite women standing across from him. He hadn't worked the courage up yet to even tell himself that he had more feelings for Susan than a simple doctor-nurse relationship.

Susan knew from the rosy color that had now reached his forehead, exactly what Josh was feeling. Even with a mask on, she smiled and murmured, "Damn right you couldn't have. Now get out of here and eat something. I'll yell if I need you."

Josh grumbled that he could survive the lack of food once in a while even as a smile broke out on his face as he turned and walked out the door.

Susan continued to clean the small surgical site then checked Rusty's blood pressure. Finally satisfied that the younger woman was resting comfortably, she turned to Griffin who was sitting in a folding metal chair at the end of the table.

He had managed to remain in the room during the surgery, but had quickly discovered that Rusty bleeding was not something he dealt well with. Oddly, it didn't make him sick or queasy. A rage so violent that it shocked him even as he contemplated ways to maim and hurt the person that had done this Rusty.

Susan, mistaking Griffin's silence for worry and shame, smiled as she tucked a blanket around Rusty.

"She's lucky to have you Griffin, even if you can't stand the sight of blood. Now why don't you pull that chair over here and hold her hand. She'll know you're here and that's what matters.

I'll go grab us some coffee and we'll sit and watch over her. I'd better check on Josh too. Damn fool probably forgot to eat. It's a good thing God threw us all together; it's just too bad he couldn't have let us keep the hot water tanks. A hot bath would be a little piece of heaven right now."

She quietly stepped out of the room, closing the door behind her.

Griffin was still in the stranglehold rage and wasn't able to speak. Still, he did stand and move the chair around to the other end of the table, closer to Rusty's head. He reached for her hand and saw his own shaking.

He stood and watched it shake for a moment, then slowly forming a fist, he whirled and smashed his hand into the wall behind him. The kerosene lamp rattled on the wall, but remained attached.

His forehead pressed against the cool plaster, one hand spread out on the wall beside his head, the other still tight in a fist, resting in a hole of cracked and crumbling drywall. When his breathing had slowed and he couldn't feel his pulse pounding behind his eyes, he turned and sat in the chair beside the operating table.

Gently reaching up he laid a hand over Rusty's cheek. Lightly caressing, he whispered in her ear, "I'm here Rusty. You're going to be alright. No one will ever hurt you again as long as I have a breath in my body, I swear it."

Chapter seven

When the group had discovered the old farm house, Josh had quickly announced that the office in the center of the structure would be the medical facility. Now after having been at the farm for a little over a year, people from the outlying area had heard there was a real doctor to be had. Josh was kept busy with an assortment of injuries and ailments on a daily basis. Patients usually paid in some sort of trade as money was useless. Money didn't feed you or keep the winter winds at bay, but a freshly weaned piglet or a bushel basket of apples went a ways to keeping the group healthy.

The office had been refurbished as items had been scavenged from the nearest town. The town, New Springs, had been a small retirement community, complete with an eighteen-hole golf course and nursing home. Within a month of the EMP more than half of the city's population had died from health issues. Pacemakers had stopped instantly at the terrorist attack, insulin was no longer mailed to homes, kidneys needing dialysis failed, and O2 machines stopped working when the gasoline powered generators ran out of fuel.

One year ago the small clan had reached the town. Josh Martin had been at a medical conference in Oklahoma when the Sun changed life for the world. He had intended to try to get back to Kansas City, when he had run into Rusty, Kevin and Griffin just outside of Wichita. They had informed him that that city was under martial law and was not allowing anyone in or out of the city limits. Deciding to travel together for safety purposes, the small group was joined by each of its current members one by one.

Just as winter was closing in on the group, they found shelter in one of New Spring, Missouri's churches. Dawson and Kevin came back the next morning after a recon of the town with news of a house just on the outskirts of the city limits. There was a hand-pump water well and an honest-to-goodness cast-iron stove in the kitchen. Apparently the house had been kept in its original 1880's design, hence the National Registry plaque.

Having survived the winter, crops had been planted using antique trackers and mule drawn plow. The farm was well guarded from theft by around the clock sentries. Anyone that came to the farm and asked was given food, shelter or medical attention. The foolish ones that tried to steal though were met with rifles, shotguns, arrows and even cast iron skillets. Word spread quickly throughout the region that New Springs just wasn't worth the trouble.

Chapter eight

"I'm not going to carry a gun!" Rusty turned, shaking her head in frustration and walked away from Griffin.

He had met her in the barnyard out back of the house. He, on his way from the west field of wheat, she, going to open the south gate to let the goats into the barnyard for evening milking.

He had broached the subject of Rusty carrying a gun for the last two weeks. As soon as she had been released to go back to work from Josh, Griff had brought it up almost daily, and Rusty refused, adamantly.

As he watched her walk away, he muttered to himself about pig-headed women.

Josh had stepped out of the back door of the house, stopping for a moment to enjoy the sun on his face. He had just finished with the sick and wounded walk-ins for the day.

He had seen Rusty and Griffin meet in the yard. Both had smiles for the other and a slow, savored kiss followed with a brief hug. As Josh watched, Griffin said something to Rusty. The smile faded from her face, replaced with a frown and a grimace. Clearly annoyed, Rusty shook her head, spoke sharply and pivoted on a heel, walking quickly away from Griffin.

Josh slowly came down the steps of the porch, still watching the two. As he neared Griffin, the younger man turned at the sound of gravel crunching underfoot.

"Josh, she just won't listen to reason! I told her there was no way she was going out to look for supplies unless she carried a gun!" Looking back at Rusty, who was now luring one of the goats up on to the milking table with a bucket of grain, he reached up and grasped his head and growled in frustration.

Josh hid his chuckle behind his hand before rubbing his hand over razor stubble on his chin.

"Won't listen to reason, or won't take orders from you?" He said with a small smile.

"Same thing isn't it? You know I'm right. I won't let her get hurt again, hell I shouldn't even let her out of the house. She's too reckless!"

"I wouldn't go so far as reckless. Now, head-strong maybe... obstinate, totally stubborn. I could think of someone else who matches that description. In fact, he's standing right in front of me acting like a damn fool."

Griffin opened his mouth to object, but Josh held his hand up to silence him.

"Griffin, your problem is you're telling her to do something she doesn't want to do. She's not a soldier in case you haven't noticed, and she sure as hell doesn't consider you her commander."

Griffin's mouth opened again, but a look from Josh shut it just as quickly.

"You love her and you don't want her hurt again, I get that. But I also get that she is a very independent young woman that is facing a very challenging world right now.

"She has seen and done things in the past year that she would have never dreamed she'd be doing in this lifetime. She wants to be strong and able to face this new world. She'll walk beside you anywhere you want to go Griffin.

"Now, listen to me. I said she would walk beside you, but she'll never be happy walking behind you. She is your equal. You can't order her around and expect her to jump through hoops for you. You'll lose her faster than you can blink if you try."

Griffin, blew air out of puffed cheeks and shoved his hands in his front pockets of his jeans.

"Doc, I hear you, and you're right. But the last two weeks…God, I almost lost her! I keep seeing her lying there, bleeding. I don't know what I'd do if she was gone. What'll I do? Let her go off and get herself killed so she can prove she's as bad ass as me?"

"You're bad ass, huh?" Josh's eye brows raised in question.

"You know what I mean!" Griffin scowled.

Josh raised a hand in surrender, even as he chuckled. "You're right, I do. Tell, you what. I'll talk to Rusty."

Chapter nine

Rusty sat on the surgery table, legs swinging.

"So I can go out on trips again, right? I'm going stir crazy here, if I have to milk that crazy Tulip goat another day, we may have roasted goat for supper. I always thought goats were sweet! The ones at the zoo were, but she's mean!"

Josh chuckled as he finished writing in Rusty's chart. He was fairly sure that Tulip the goat was just as anxious to send Rusty elsewhere. The young woman just didn't have the knack for milking goats. Both participants seemed cranky when all was said and done.

"Tell you what, I'll give you a clean bill of health if you promise to take it easy out there, and secondly, I want you to start carrying a gun. Now don't get your panties in a bunch, I know all about you refusing to carry a weapon, I've talked with Griffin."

Rusty blurted, "I can't believe you're siding with him! You've taken an oath to save lives, not take them, Josh!"

The physician continued, "I am a doctor, Rusty, but I was a solider first. I took that oath, and don't think I don't take it serious, I do. At the same time, I am not foolish enough to stand by and let mine be harmed by the actions of others.

"I also know that there have been more and more reports coming in from the outlying farms of small bands of rabble moving through the area. You were lucky you only met up with two of them. Think about what could have happened to you, Rusty. Think good and hard on it. You've seen firsthand what comes into the clinic after those animals have finished with a farm."

Rusty had indeed seen. She shuddered at the memory of the mother and daughter that had been raped by one of the packs of wild animals that posed as human. Josh had done everything medical he could for both of them.

Unfortunately, not everything broken could be mended. Last she had heard the young girl still hadn't spoken a word. Her mother had found sanctuary deep in her mind, unable to do anything but sit and rock by a window. The husband and father of the two, at his wit's end, had recently taken in a family that had escaped one of the cities to help with the farm and to care for his wife and daughter.

"Furthermore, think about why Griffin has been in your face about this. It's not because he wants to boss you around…"

"I get it. He wants me safe, I know. Although, yes he is very bossy. Okay, Josh, I'll carry a gun. There's just one thing. I…" Rusty's face grew red, her arms defensively crossed in front of her body.

Josh looked expectantly at her even as she grew more uncomfortable.

"You've handled firearms before haven't you? Didn't you need to know how to shoot a tranq gun at the zoo?"

"Well, yeah, but shooting a needle full of tranquilizer at a tiger is a little different than shooting bullets at human! I don't know if I can do it Josh! What if I freeze up and can't do it? What if I get one of us killed, because they think I've got their back?"

Nodding his head in understanding, Josh walked up to the young woman and laid his hands on her shoulders. Catching her eye, he gave her a small smile.

"Rusty, there is no one I would trust more with my own life than you. You may doubt yourself now at this minute, but when the day comes and you have no choice but to choose between saving one of us or letting some slime ball win…well, it's a no-brainer. You'll step up, girl, don't worry."

Chapter ten

After supper had been eaten and cleaned up, Griffin and Rusty walked out to the pond a half mile past the barn. Walking hand in hand through the tall grasses the two enjoyed the silence of easy companionship.

Rusty had taken to heart the job of learning how to shoot well. She practiced with Dawson or Josh daily. She and Josh had forbade Griffin from taking part in the sessions.

Rusty didn't take orders well, and for Griffin to be issuing them would have been counter-productive. So to save the peace and possibly Griffin's health the two other men had taken the task.

"Dawson told me you were doing great with shooting. He said, 'If she keeps it up, she'll be shooting the side of a mile-wide barn in no time!'"

He laughed as Rusty jabbed him in the side with her elbow. Taking her arm, he pulled it to settle on his hips then draped his over her shoulders, hugging her gently.

"He did say that, but he was joking. He said you were a natural. One of those people that can point a gun like you were pointing your finger and hit the target every time."

"Well, like I told Josh, that target doesn't move, breath or bleed either. Pretty easy to shoot at a bottle or piece of paper."

Snatching a sunflower as they walked past it, Rusty studied the yellow and orange petals.

"I had a clay pitcher sitting on my table, back in my apartment. It had sunflowers painted on it. I'd stop by the corner market every Friday and pick up fresh cut flowers. They always looked so pretty." She was silent for a few minutes.

"Do you think life will ever be normal again? I miss hot showers, and the radio. Not so much the radio, but music. I was humming the other day and just started crying because I couldn't remember the words to "Hey, Delilah". It's stupid, I know."

They walked on, reached the pond and sat on the old log that was there for sitting. The frogs croaked and fish slapped the surface as they hunted insects.

"Chinese take-out. Dryer sheets. Oh, and porn." Griffin grinned at the last missed item.

"Gross! You are such a sick puppy! The world has ended and you miss porn!" He also had pulled Rusty out of her funk and she was grateful.

"I think we'll get it all back. We lost the technology, but we haven't lost the people that know how to create it again. The government probably whisked all those Smarticles off to safe bunkers until all the lunatics killed each other off. A few more years of "Little House on the Prairie" and we'll be back to "Sex in the City," never fear." Griffin looked out over the pond, then turned and looked at Rusty.

"The question is, will you be Laura or Carrie when the time comes?"

"Oh, no worries there! I can walk away from butter churning and goat milking anytime. Not sure I'm willing to switch to high heels and high fashion dresses though. I just want my lions and tigers back.

"What do you suppose happened to our animals, Griff? Do you wonder?" Her whimsical smile from fashion statements faded away as she thought about the many animals in the zoo that she herself had abandoned to go find her brother.

"I have wondered. I know the older two girls in the elephant house were probably put down early on. They wouldn't have lasted the winter with those old bones. I hope someone chose to put all the animals down that couldn't be fed or couldn't be turned loose to fend for themselves."

"Yeah. I figure mine are all dead. I would hope so at least. I hate to say that, but can you imagine going to get a deer you just shot and Bruno beats you to it?"

Bruno the majestic Siberian Tiger that lived at the Kansas City Zoo was a huge cat. At five years old, he had been the largest tiger in captivity on record. He was also the most surly and sneaky cat that ever lived. His entire goal in life had been to mate, eat and try and kill any human that came within reach.

A shudder went through Griffin as he pictured the scene Rusty had just painted. "Let's hope they're gone then."

The serenity of the pond was broken. Day had given over to night and shadows crept in from the surrounding trees. Lions, tigers and whatever slid through the night seemed to make up the darkness, causing goose bumps to prickle Rusty's arms.

"Let's go home." She stood, taking Griffin's hand and led him back down the path to the house with lantern-lit windows beckoning them towards safety.

Chapter eleven

He watched them from the darkness of the trees. Twice he took a step to show himself. Twice he stopped himself. He needed to find help soon, but would these people help or would they hurt?

The couple rose and began walking back down the worn path towards the house.

He had watched them walk down to the pond, had observed them talking but couldn't hear any of their conversation.

He had seen the girl before, had seen her in that town. She had hurt Virgil. It had made him sad, but he had had to protect his friend. Virgil protected him all the time.

Virgil said that they couldn't be mad at the girl, so he wasn't. Virgil was terrible hurt though. He had to be a man and find help for Virgil. He was afraid Virgil would die, like his momma had died. If Virgil died, he would be all alone again. It was scary to be alone.

It was getting dark in the trees. He needed to go back and put more wood on the fire so Virgil wouldn't get cold in the night. He would tell him about the other boy and the girl that he had watched at the pond. Virgil would know what to do.

Noiselessly, the man turned into the woods and walked without making a sound.

Chapter twelve

The backdoor opened into the kitchen, Susan walked in with an empty basket.

"That's two days in a row that there weren't any eggs. Do you think we have a bull snake in the chicken coop?" Moving to the counter across from Rusty who was cutting out biscuits from the dough in front of her.

Pushing the drinking glass down into the dough in a row of five, Rusty glanced up, a frown of consternation marked her face.

"It would have to be a really big snake or a herd of them. We usually find a dozen eggs or more every morning. Maybe something is wrong with the chickens? Are they acting differently? I heard the rooster this morning, well before daylight I might add. I really hate that bird."

Spoken with no malice, everyone knew that Rusty had a soft spot for the Rhode Island Red rooster; she just liked sleeping also.

"Maybe you should let Josh know. Now that I think about it, Dawson said half of the apples we picked yesterday were missing. I figured the kids must be snagging them, I wonder if anything else is missing."

Joey and Thomas burst into the room, one yelling and demanding justice after being wrongly accused by the other.

Susan sat both the boys down and made them slow down and discuss what had happened as people started filtering in for breakfast.

Rusty pulled a sheet of biscuits out of the warming oven and slid the raw dough into the oven.

Dawson came in and helped bring the biscuits, gravy, bacon, spiced apples, and jellies and butter over to the table.

Once the meal was being enjoyed by all, the missing eggs and apples were brought to Josh's attention.

"Alright folks, looks like we are going back to around-the-clock sentries. I'll post the schedule this afternoon. Griffin, why don't you take the first watch tonight until one. Dawson, you take the one to six slot. Both of you get some rest this afternoon. We'll get someone else to work the fields and man the front gate to cover for you.

If any of you see anything suspicious, don't go off by yourself to investigate! Groups of three or more, especially you women, and you're all to carry weapons. I think the children should stay near the house until we get to the bottom of this."

It was a perfect late summer day. Several of the men and women went out to the apple orchard and gathered more of the red fruit, beating the birds to several bushel baskets before mid-morning.

Colleen and Frank went into the surrounding woods to see about shooting a deer or two. Two large bucks had been seen fighting for the rights of a harem of does at the pond earlier in the week.

With any luck, Colleen would bring down at least two deer with her compound bow and steel tipped arrows.

Winter was looming closer each day, food was imperative for the groups survival, as was wood for fuel. The sound of ax to wood rang behind the barn. Several large dead-fall trees had be dragged closer to the house by Trixie and Penn, the enormous, matched, gray dappled draft horses that resided at Fort Repose.

Trixie and Penn had both been found at the front gate one morning a few months after the group had first arrived. Both had been tethered to the metal post, a bag of grooming supplies and a piece of paper with the horse's names scrawled on it, but no clue as to who had gifted the farm with the horses.

It had been assumed that the owner had not been able to feed the horses in the coming winter and had chosen to give them a better chance for survival.

Livestock had become a favored choice of payment for many of the areas' inhabitants. Feed was hard to come by with the local CO-OP no longer in existence. Fort Repose had the ability to grow and harvest food for man and beast because of the antique implements found in the barn.

But even Fort Repose had its limitations. So, some of the animals were once again traded for other needed items or were used to feed the group that had reached fifteen in number now.

Several people in the kitchen were canning fruits and vegetables for the coming cold months. The opened windows, curtains fluttering in and out, caught what breeze there was, bringing little relief. The wood stove was putting out an unbelievable amount of heat. Two canners boiled away on the stovetop with jars of spiced apples and apple sauce.

Tobias Edwards was at the table preparing apples for drying. He was expounding the glorious uses of dried apples to Susan, Kate, Rusty and Missy.

"My grandparents had an apple orchard in Washington State. Raised Granny Smiths, Braeburns, and Galas. Grandma Williams would dry apples for the winter. She would can too, never took stock in the freezing anything. Always said electricity was too unreliable….guess she was right." He chuckled at the irony of it.

"Anyhow, I spent a winter with them when I was, oh, about the same age as you Missy. Yeah, I was almost sixteen and chomping at the bit to go out and be a man.

"That's why I ended up out in Washington that winter. Seems I thought I was old enough to try and join the Army. Vietnam was getting hot and heavy on the TV and radio, and I was hopping mad that the Army and my parents thought I was too young.

"My parents sent me out to the farm to keep my mind away from the war. Grandpap wouldn't buy a television and the radio didn't work most of the time. So I was stuck fifty miles out in the Washington backwoods all winter. When I wasn't chopping wood, I was learning to cook with Grandma.

"She made apple pie, apple dumplings, pork chops with apple sauce, apple chutney and the best apple cake in the whole world. She cooked with apples all winter and all of them were either canned or dried."

"Didn't you go to school Mr. Edwards?" Missy asked. She missed her school back at Branson Central.

"Well, I tell ya, remember I said we were out in the middle of a forest? The nearest school was in Timberton and it was close to fifty miles. No, no school, but plenty of learning. Grandma had taught my daddy the same as she taught me that winter. I probably learned more that year than any other year in a real school. She was a strict teacher, I'll tell you what!"

"Speaking of schooling. I believe you have an essay due today on the American Revolution. I'm anxious to read about you Yanks kicking some English bum. We only were taught the English side of the fight you know." Kate Blackman's Irish accent was light and bubbly and directed at Missy.

"I finished, Kate! I also finished the math assignment. I think you need to bump me up a level or two in math, this was so easy!" Missy chirped.

Kate laughed and shook her head, "If you could convince your brother and Tommy that school is fun, I would give you an A for sure! Those two remind me of my little brother growing up. He would give the school master fits daily. Ah, but they're young and the world is so much better outside of a schoolroom, to be sure."

Tears welled in Kate's eyes, surprising her. She laughed as she wiped them away with her apron.

"Well! That caught me a bit off guard! I haven't just started crying like that for a few months now. I suppose thinking of William is to blame. He was a beastly little brother when we were children, but he did grow into a fine young man. He would fall down laughing to see me now."

Missy laughed, but looked questioningly at Kate.

"Ha! Beastly! I can think of another little brother that matches that description! Joey drives me to distraction most of the time! Why would your brother laugh at you now?"

"Well, you have to have known me in Ireland. I owned a small bed and breakfast just on the edge of Belfast. I had a lovely little flower garden that I paid a man to care for. You see, I was never the sort to be at one with the earth, you might say. So, if William could see me now, out climbing apple trees and helping to mulch a ten acre garden. Mud under my nails and dirt ground into my knees! He would enjoy seeing me out of my element. You know what? I wish he could see me now, I've changed. I'm tougher than I was then, before. I think we all are."

Kate missed her little brother immensely, and prayed each day that he and her mum and da were handling this new life. Right after the solar flare, she had been frantic, wishing daily she had stayed home in Ireland instead of "hopping over the pond" to visit her friend, Susan Fraser.

If she had declined Susan's invitation to explore the Ozarks, she would be close to her parents and younger brother and, well, home. She hoped her bed and breakfast was being used; the thought of it sitting empty seemed a waste.

As time passed however, she had claimed this motley group of Americans as her family. She may not ever see her blood family again, but she would still be accepted into this group as a sister, and she felt some peace knowing that.

Just as the last jar of apple sauce was being pulled from the water bath canner, a shout from outside pulled everyone from the kitchen and out into the farm yard.

Rusty, the last out of the house, saw Frank pulling the deer sled loaded with a huge buck into the yard. It was the other canvas sled, being pulled by a stranger, which drew her attention.

Colleen walked slightly behind the stranger and was talking to another man who was lying on the sled.

"Got a sick one here, Doc!" Colleen looked past the group of people to Josh who had just walked out of the barn.

Frank dragged the dead deer on into the barn, calling for Joey and Thomas to help him hang the carcass. Both boys walked slowly in, dragging their feet, heads turned back to watch Josh squat down to examine the man.

Rusty stood in the center of the yard. The words "fever and infection" floated past her, but all she could really focus on was the man standing still as a statue, still wearing the harness that was attached to the sled.

His hair, dark brown, long and greasy was tucked behind his ears. He wore holey, once blue, jeans, held up by a length of rope. The twine peeked out from under an equally holey tee shirt and a ragged pair of tennis shoes.

He was panting from the exertion of pulling, looking down at the ground. Slowly he looked up, scanning his surroundings. His gaze stopped at Rusty.

Rusty's lungs froze and refused to draw in air. Even at a distance, she could see the colors of his eyes. One brown, the other as blue as the sky they stood under.

Chapter thirteen

He was tired, scared. Virgil had moaned all through last night, keeping sleep from them both. He had been so frightened that if he fell asleep, Virgil would be dead when he woke.

Early this morning, after trying to feed Virgil a bit of cooked egg and failing, he had heard voices deeper in the forest.

Virgil had whispered to him to go get help. He'd been afraid, but had done as his friend asked.

A man and woman were standing over a deer in a small clearing.

The deer was lying in the soft grass, surrounded by tiny yellow flowers, an arrow shaft protruding from its side.

The man saw him first, and swung a rifle off his shoulder to hold, ready.

"Howdy", the man said, drawing the woman's attention away from the deer she had just knelt beside.

She stood, drawing an arrow from her quiver on her back, smoothly notching it to the string of the compound bow in her left hand.

He paused for a moment, frightened, then remembered that he needed to help Virgil, and walked slowly towards the couple.

The man with the rifle was scanning the trees around the glade, looking for anything threatening.

The woman spoke, her voice soft and clear, "We aren't looking for trouble Mister, I hope you don't plan on bringing us any."

He shook his head, trying to get the words out of his brain into his mouth.

"No! Help...I..No...Virgil." He stopped, frustrated with his tongue. "Virgil needs help. Virgil is sick. I can't get him to eat. Hot...Virgil is real hot. Momma got real hot, then she left me."

"Wait. Easy there son; you have someone who's sick? Where is he? Are you alone?" The man kept the rifle in a relaxed position, but didn't lower it completely.

The woman took a step closer to him, "Virgil, your friend, he needs help? Can you show us?"

"Easy Colleen, this could be a trap. Might be others out there." The man with the rifle spoke as he raised the gun.

Colleen stopped and put her hand softly on the rifle barrel and pushed it down.

"No, it's okay Frank, look at him... listen to him. He's what my daddy would call 'special'." She turned back and smiled at the stranger then, and he relaxed.

Momma had always told him he was a special boy, and *she* loved him. This woman must be nice.

"Come on, Virgil needs me to come back. Virgil needs help." He turned his back to the couple and walked a few steps into the trees. Turning, he beckoned them to follow.

Not far off an old animal trail, was the camp. Virgil was struggling to rise from the pallet of blankets, as they came through the trees.

Colleen rushed over as Virgil's strength failed and eased his head back down to the ground.

"Frank, he's burning up with fever. We need to get him to Doc."

It was discussed and decided that Frank and the boy would go back and get the deer while Colleen readied the sick man for travel.

Once back with the deer, the boy had insisted that he pull Virgil back to the house.

Colleen helped him into the harness that was attached to the sled before she spoke.

"Can you tell me your name?" She smiled as she spoke; the boy was obviously scared. He acted as if he were a puppy that had been kicked one too many times. Her heart hurt at the thought. *Had* he been beaten in the past?

She reached up to put a comforting hand on his shoulder. As she touched him he flinched slightly, his head down, breath coming in short, little gasps.

"Hey, we won't hurt you, I promise. You were very smart and brave to come get us."

"Virgil is my friend. He said he would keep me safe."

"Let's get Virgil to the house so the doctor can look at him."

She pointed to her husband as she spoke, "Frank and I will keep you safe until Virgil feels better, okay? My name's Colleen. Can you tell me your name now?"

"Yes. My name is Zane. Momma said it means a gift from God." Zane looked shyly up at Colleen with a tiny smile.

"That's a very special name. It's nice to meet you, Zane." Colleen patted his shoulder.

Chapter fourteen

"Rusty, hand me that clean cloth will you? Rusty?" Susan looked up from the old man, waiting for the rag she needed to wipe his face.

Rusty was standing on the other side of the table staring down at the man. She swayed slightly, eyes, unblinking. Her eyebrows were drawn together with a frown, reliving the last time she had seen the old man.

Susan reached across and snapped her fingers close to Rusty's face. Rusty jumped as if bitten and her eyes flew to Susan's face.

"What? Oh, sorry; here." Her face reddened as she handed the soft cloth over to the other woman.

The man moaned softly as Susan gently blotted his dirt streaked face. She could feel the heat pouring off of him, she wondered how long he could hold on.

Josh had examined him just a short time ago. He had pulled Susan out in the hall to speak.

"He has the classic symptoms of a ruptured appendix. I would almost guess that it burst sometime in the past two or three days."

"I've got Cipro dissolved in his I.V. I hate to say it, it was probably a waste of our last antibiotics. . It's only a matter of hours now, the peritonitis has gone too far."

"If the pain becomes too much for him, we can help with that at least. Keeping him comfortable is all we can do now."

He shook his head in frustration. Knowing he could have saved this life two years ago, and not being able to do so now weighed heavily on him.

"What about the young man? Zane. How is he going to handle this?" Susan murmured, her heart heavy for the poor soul who was now in the kitchen being fed by Kate.

Josh wondered that himself. The mentioned young man showed mild to moderate IDD, (Intellectual development disorder). A century ago people like Zane had been called feeble minded or simple and were institutionalized and forgotten by society. In the last decade, the world had been opened up to these people with special needs. They blended with the rest of humanity. Now though, this was a different, sometimes violent world. A world where being different was not necessarily a good thing.

"We'll just have to help him handle whatever comes. We can be his family now. I'll go talk to him; yell if anything changes in there."

Rusty was helping Susan clean the man when his eyes opened. They looked up first Susan and over to Rusty. Surprised, Rusty backed a step. The man's hand suddenly shot out and grabbed her arm.

Rusty was startled by the strength of the grip, looking from the hand holding her, back to his face.

He tried to speak, but coughed instead. He moaned in pain, but managed to speak,

"He didn't mean no harm, ya gotta believe that. He had forgotten he had the knife in his hand. We had been in the storeroom…" A spasm of pain had him grimacing, breathing shallowly until the wave passed.

"He'd been prying at a box with it. Just forgot he had it is all. Then you," He laughed then. "You were a feisty one. He thought you meant real harm to me, ya see? He only meant to hit ya, he was scared and he forgot he had the knife… Promise me you'll do right by him. He's all alone in this messed up world now."

His gripped tightened, causing Rusty to wince.

"Promise me…please." The pleading note in his voice broke through whatever barrier Rusty had.

"Yes, of course…of course we will." She tried to smile.

"You just rest now, don't you worry about the boy, he has a home here now." Susan took hold of his other hand and shook it gently. She looked across to Rusty, a question in her eyes?

This was one of the men that had attacked you?

Rusty nodded slightly.

Yes.

The man was able to tell the two women that his name was Virgil Trudell. He was, or had been the bus driver for The Ozark Valley Friends, a nonprofit organization that created job opportunities for people, like Zane Hackett, with IDD.

Virgil had taken Zane in after Zane's mother had passed away shortly after the solar flare. Zane was thirty two, but had the mentality of an eight year old.

Both had been living off the land for months after a group of bikers had chased them from Virgil's home.

Virgil had grown up running wild in the Ozark hills, though, and found that doing so again hadn't been much of a hardship.

"That boy loves to grow things. You give him a plot of ground and some seeds and he can feed an army. He won't be a burden, that's for sure. Just one thing, if you have a storm come in, one with lots of thunder, watch him. He's scairt to death of those boomers."

The fever seemed to take hold of Trudell that afternoon. He was able to talk to Zane, reassuring the young man that he would be taken care of here, before he slipped into a coma-like sleep.

Rusty was sitting with the old man that night. The house was still and quiet around her. The last thumping up the stairs to the bedrooms had been over an hour before. She had wanted to sit with him, not wanting him to be alone.

Josh had been in with his patient, knowing the man was on the verge of death. He had stepped out a few minutes ago to make coffee.

Rusty had visited with Zane that afternoon. She had tried her best to make him feel at ease around her. It would take some time though. Both remembered their first encounter too well.

She knew that it really had been an accident... that Zane hadn't meant to hurt her, just stop her from hurting his friend.

While talking with him, she had discovered that he had raised goats when he was with his mother. He had smiled and bounced from foot to foot with excitement when she had told him that the farm had goats that needed milking twice a day and lots of attention. She had been almost as excited as Zane at the thought of pawning cantankerous goats off on someone else!

Virgil's breathing was becoming slower and more labored. Rusty reached up and held the man's hand, hoping he knew he wasn't alone.

Josh quietly entered the room, two mugs of steaming coffee in his hands. As he handed Rusty a cup, he studied the man on the table. He took the free hand and found the weak pulse. Looking over at Rusty, he shook his head.

They sat quietly, drinking coffee, content with each other's presence.

Suddenly, Virgil took a shuddering breath, released it and was silent.

Rusty tensed, waiting for the next breath that wouldn't ever come.

Josh stood, taking his stethoscope to the man's chest for several seconds. He straightened, sighed and laid a hand gently over Rusty's hand still grasping the old man's.

"He's gone. May he find peace."

Rusty's eyes filled, she felt a great sadness for Virgil, but Zane was the reason for her tears.

"Zane. He's lost so much already. He shouldn't have to lose any more. It's just not fair is it?"

She let Josh wrap his arms around her and she cried. She cried for Zane and she cried for herself. Life had become so hard, so difficult. She wanted her old life back. She knew she was feeling sorry for herself, but that didn't stop the tears from flowing. Finally, she gained control again, laughing in dismay at the big wet splotch on Josh's shirt.

"You know, I knew a nurse a few years back that was amazing in the ER. She never got flustered, wouldn't back down from anything. She faced blood, violence and hysteria every single day. Nothing seem to faze her. Then one day, she didn't show up for her shift. She didn't answer her phone. So, after the shift, one of the other nurses and an orderly went over to her apartment."

"They found her on her bed. Her apartment was all packed up. She had left instructions for everything she owned to be donated. She had OD'ed on sleeping pills. She left a note. In it she said she was tired of not feeling. You see, she saw life and death every day, and she was the perfect nurse, but she had forgotten how to see the simple joys in life. Maybe forgotten is the wrong word. I think she wasn't able to feel the emotions we take for granted. She didn't feel the happiness of seeing a baby breathe its first breath. She didn't feel grief when a young couple died in a car accident. She knew she didn't feel anything, and finally I think she grew tired of it."

"Don't ever give up your emotions, Rusty. Rejoice in the fact that you do grieve. Sadness is just as important in life as happiness, because we need both. Life isn't balanced otherwise."

"I think Virgil here had a good life. He would appreciate the tears, but he would want you to smile when you wake up tomorrow. Now, why don't you head on upstairs. I'm sure Griffin is missing your snoring about now."

Rusty hiccupped a laugh and playfully punched Josh's arm, "I do not snore! Seriously though, thank you, Josh."

Now alone with the old man, Josh gently pulled the sheet up over Virgil's head. Tomorrow he and the other members of the house would gather and lay him to rest. He hoped when his time came, he had someone to do the same for him.

Chapter fifteen

Griffin walked into the barn and the whispering in the back horse stall stopped. His mouth twitched with a smile as he continued deeper into the barn to see what the boys were up to.

As he approached the stall, Zane stepped out of the enclosure with a decidedly guilty look on his face. He put his elbow up to rest on the front pole of the stall, trying to block Griffin's view.

"Hi'ya Griff!" The exuberant greeting was followed with a blush and smile.

The man had been cleaned up and fed properly the past two months. His long, greasy hair had been washed and cut and new clothes had be scrounged up for him, making him much more presentable in body and spirit.

He worked himself hard, wanting to do just as much as the other men on the farm, but he was drawn to the boys. If he was not needed in the fields after the milking and morning chores were done, he could be found, more times than not, with Joey and Thomas.

They made a fort on the edge of the woods, had hung a tire and rope from the ancient cottonwood tree by the pond and had all ended up in bed early one night, after eating too many strawberries from the garden, with stomach aches.

Zane was part of the family now, in his eyes and the groups. He still grieved for his friend now and again, but was happy where he was now.

"I was looking for Thomas and Joey, have you seen them? They were supposed to help clean the back goat shed today. I was just there and it's still piled with junk." Griffin was fairly sure that the two boys were behind Zane.

There was rustling of hay, a thump, and a whispered "Ouch" that brought the smile out full force on Griffin.

"So, what'cha got back there, boys?" He patiently waited, and was rewarded by a voice in the shadowy corner.

"It's okay Zane, let him see." Thomas peeked out from under Zane's arm that still rested on the post.

Zane's smile turned up brighter than before and turned, giving Griffin a view of two boys, hunkered down in the hay.

Zane spoke, excitement radiating out, "Tommy and Joey found it in the shed! We can keep it, right?"

Griffin stepped into the stall and squatted down to get a closer look at object of the excitement. The boys moved away from the moving object so Griff could see.

As his eyes adjusted to the dim light, they widened in surprise as a small growl followed by a hiss came from the straw nest.

"Well, I'll be. Boys, you've got yourselves a real live African lion cub!" Even as he spoke, a cold chill ran down his back.

"You said you found it in the back shed? Was this the only one?" As he spoke, he scooped up the three to four week old cub. Holding it by the nap of its neck, just as the mother lion would, he looked it over.

She hung limply, which was natural; this was the way the mother would transport it. Dark blue, slanted eyes where slits. Its tan, spotted body shivered in the hot air. Griffin ran a hand down the length of its little body and wasn't surprised to feel bones instead of baby fat. This baby had been abandoned or something had happened to the mother.

"Boys, I think we need to take this little girl in the house and try and get some warm milk in her belly. First things first though. She may be sick, so I want all of you to go wash your hands with lots of soap and water.

"After you have washed, go find Rusty, I think she is out front with Dawson. She's the big cat expert. Also, I don't want you anywhere out of the yard. Until we find out what has happened to this one's mama, we need to assume she's out there looking for her baby. Lion moms are not friendly like our barn cats."

Griffin was seated by the wood stove, trying to get the small cub to lap milk from a dish, when Rusty burst through the front door with all three of the boys, all of them thundered down the hall to the kitchen and burst into the room.

"They really found a lion cub? Ahhh, it is isn't it! Is it a girl or boy? Come here little baby, let me see you." Rusty's machine gun questions and girly cooing caused Griffin to burst out laughing.

That adorable smile on Rusty's face wasn't seen much these days. The thought jolted Griffin. He would just have to start bringing her baby animals more often, he decided.

"She's about four weeks old, but she's very dehydrated and malnourished. Yes you are, sweet thing."

"We can keep her, right Rusty? She can sleep in my room, I don't mind!" Zane was obviously as much in love as Rusty.

"Mom, can I sleep in Zane's room from now on?" Thomas immediately asked his mother as she walked into the kitchen, drawn by the voices.

"Me too, Zane! Dad won't mind!" Joey joined in.

Before Colleen could agree or veto, Griffin held up his hand to silence everyone.

"I think Rusty needs to examine the cub before anything is decided. Colleen? We possibly have a sick or wounded mother African lion roaming the farm. We need to let everyone know as quickly as we can. If we see it, we need to take it down, no hesitation."

Colleen nodded and went out the door leading to the barnyard, Tommy, Joey and Zane in tow.

A comfortable silence settled in the kitchen. Tobias Edwards, the cook for the day, continued to peel potatoes at the long wooden table, not concerned at all that a wild animal was in the house.

"She's awfully weak, Griff. I don't think she stands much of a chance. Who knows when she suckled last? Honestly, it's for the best if she doesn't make it really. What would we do with a lion?" Rusty had been looking down at the baby on her lap, gently stroking the downy fur.

Tobias spoke up, "I remember having a coyote pup when I was a kid. I found it out by the old highway, you know, ol' 97. Its mother had been hit by a car. Found it huddled up against her. So I brung home this pup, I raised it, trained it to fetch and sit up, all the things you teach a dog. But it chased the chickens, ended up getting in the coop and killing every one of mother's laying hens. Pa ended up shooting it."

He continued peeling spuds as he reminisced, "Pa sat me down, me bawling like a big ol baby, and told me that me and that coyote had just been pretending. I guess he was right."

"What were you pretending, Tobias?" Griffin looked over at the old man, a quizzical look on his face.

"I asked him that too." Tobias chuckled, "Me and the coyote had convinced ourselves that it was a dog. Just a plain ol' dog. We forgot where he'd come from. So, one day the wildness in him just jumped out and got him by the throat. He was made to chase his food, not wait for it to be put down in front of him in a pretty bowl. He chased and killed those chickens cuz God put him on the Earth to do things like that."

"I know what you're saying, Tobias, and your right. This cub doesn't have a place here, because someday down the road she would remember that she was a lion. I don't think we'll have to worry about it though. Look at her."

The small creature being talked about had given up. Its mother was gone and it knew it, somehow. Now it simply waited. Even as the small group had talked, the little cub's breaths had grown shorter and less frequent.

As Rusty and Griffin sat quietly stroking the soft fur, the cub stopped moving. A tear fell from Rusty's eye and dropped on to the small body. The tear perched on a point of fur and then disappeared, sucked up by the fuzzy down.

The boys in typical boy-fashion were sad about the cub's death for all of one hour. Then the thought that a full grown lion might just be roaming the farm land, had all three of them wanting to go hunting. The adults quickly put this idea high on a top shelf, much to the boys' chagrin.

That night at the supper table the news of a lion roaming near was brought up. Drew Wilder and Frank

Payne had been out to the southeast field that afternoon, checking the cattle in that particular field. Drew spoke up when the table quieted down after the news.

"All the cattle were huddled up against the southeast corner of the pasture fence. We," he nodded at Frank, "figured it was due to a storm coming in, you know how they'll act odd right before a real leaf blower of a storm. After a head count though, we have one of the first year heifers missing, so I'm guessing the herd was spooked because of the lion. We go back out to that field, I'm guessing we'll find a carcass, maybe the lion too."

After a group consensus, a trip back out to the pasture was planned for the next morning with Colleen, Frank, Griffin, Rusty and Kevin all going fully armed.

The boys, forced to stay by the house, spent most of the day in the hayloft in the barn. There, they had a bird's eye view of the surrounding land. A pair of binoculars had been dug out of a closet, lending to quarrels of possession.

Zane had won control of the field glasses shortly after lunch. He was scanning the tree line while Joey and Tommy played with a litter of kittens behind a stack of hay bales. He was wondering how he could convince one of the other boys to take over the look out. The giggling and tiny meows behind him were sounding like much more fun than looking at boring trees.

Movement in the trees caught his attention. Looking through the lenses, he quickly let out a whoop of excitement.

"They're back! Tommy, Joey, I see'um! I see'um!"

An enthusiastic scramble down the ladder followed by much yelling, had most of the group emerging from the house. The boys and Zane were in front of the others, vying for the first glimpse of a real African lion, when the five hunters rode into the yard.

Rusty and Griffin were riding double on Penn, one of the drafts. Trixie was behind them carrying a load, covered with a tarp. Kevin, Colleen and Frank followed behind on three other horses.

Zane, Joey and Tommy were jumping all around the horses, shouting out questions.

Did they see the lion? Did the lion attack them? Why was Rusty riding with Griff? What was Trixie carrying?

"Boys, calm down! We'll tell ya'll about it after we have the horses taken care of." Frank spoke softly, but commanded the boys' attention.

"In the meantime, why don't ya'll help us? Faster we get done, the faster we can tell ya'll about it."

Tommy, Joey and Zane all rushed to unsaddle and care for the horses, tripping on each other in their haste.

Kevin and Griffin offloaded Trixie, hauling the canvas bag into the house.

Once the animals had been cared for, everyone gathered in the huge kitchen at the table.

"Alright Dad, what happened? Did you have to track the lion through heavy brush? Did you feel it breathing down your neck?" Tommy sat next to his father looking up at him with awestruck eyes.

Frank looked at Colleen and chuckled, "I think we need to cut back on Jack London books before bed for a while."

"No son, we did have to track her a bit, but there wasn't any hot breath on my collar, unless you count Kevin stepping on my heels."

"Hey! It was only the once." Kevin huffed.

Frank laughed as he cuffed Kevin on the shoulder, in a friendly way.

"No, I'm just razing ya. I have to admit to being a little nervous my own self. Tracking a deer in dense brush, that ya can't see two feet in front of ya, is one thing. Tracking a cat that can look me in the eye is another."

Colleen, hands resting on the table grasping a cup of coffee, spoke.

"I've hunted these woodlands all my life and I've never been afraid. Until today. Frank called it. It was just plum spooky out there, knowing that there was a big cat in the woods with us."

Griffin took his turn. "I'll admit I had goose bumps jump off my arms when we heard her growling. I wanted to be anywhere but there."

"Then we found them, and I just wanted to cry." Rusty spoke softly as she remembered the scene.

The group of hunters had broken out of the brushy woods to a small clearing that held a death trap. The woods were quiet all around them, taking in the life-death scene before them.

Chapter sixteen

The lioness had tried her hardest to provide for her baby. The problem was, she had never had to provide for herself. She had been hand raised by people who had given her everything she needed. Except the one thing she needed to survive this new world. They didn't give her the wildness, that very thing inside an animal that drives it to hunt for food. That thing that drives it to survive.

She and the male lion whom she had been raised with had been turned loose by their owners when horse meat stopped being delivered by refrigerated trucks. The people hadn't wanted two hungry lions in their backyard, but didn't want to put them down.

The tiny pride of lions had managed fairly well with the livestock in the area. When the easy pickings of cattle and sheep in the area were gone, the lions moved on. While winter-based in one of the many Ozark caves, the female had become pregnant.

Then earlier in the summer, the male was surprised when going after a goat. It was staked in a meadow, seemingly just waiting for the lion. It was in fact, just that. As he stalked the goat, the hunter became the hunted. Then the man in the tree stand took aim and killed the lion.

The lioness managed well on her own, providing for herself and her two small cubs born a week after their father's death. She had moved the cubs from the cave to a small out building that smelled of people. She still was drawn to what she had known for so long before.

Then, while following a deer trail at the base of a rock wall, she had been caught in a rock slide. A large rock came flying over the edge of the wall and hit her. It had shattered her jaw, and essentially destroyed her life.

Unable to kill or eat what she stalked, she became thinner and thinner. Her body couldn't produce enough milk and the cubs suffered. The smallest died one night. The hungry mewling of the remaining cub drove her out to hunt.

It had been at a mud hole, that had been a small pond earlier in the summer, she chanced upon a young heifer stuck in the mud. She had leapt onto the cow's back but managed only to gouge and claw the bellowing beast before it heaved her into the mud beside it.

The mud quickly sucked the struggling cat in. It was this scene that the group of hunters came on.

The fight, lack of water or food, and the struggle in the mud had left both beasts weak. When Frank stopped suddenly at the edge of a clearing, Kevin had run into him. Then both simply stood and stared at the sight. Colleen, Rusty and Griffin had been following behind in the tight, overgrown woods and could only hear the deep growl from somewhere in front of them, along with a weak *blah* from a cow.

Rusty spoke, the sadness she felt in her heart flowing out with the tale.

"There wasn't anything we could do for her, except put her out of her misery. I think she was relieved to see us. She just put her head down, closed her eyes and sighed." She paused for a minute, wiping her eyes with a red handkerchief that Griffin had pressed into her hand.

"She could have…no, should have, had a good life. She didn't ask to be raised by people. She should have been born in the African plains, where it wouldn't matter if the rest of the world had stopped. Her world wouldn't have changed."

In the end, both the lion and the cow had been shot. The group had managed to pull the cow out of the mud and butchered her, taking as much as they could carry back through the dense woods to the waiting horses.

The group sat around the table in silence, each one thinking how much the world had changed in the past year. They, as a group, were fortunate. Finding the farm and each other had made their lives, if not easier, safer.

A week later would prove that no one in this new world was safe.

Chapter seventeen

"Morning, birthday boy."

Griffin opened his eyes to Rusty lying on her side next to him. The bed was piled with quilts, keeping the winter cold at bay. Smiling sweetly, she slid her feet under his legs.

Griff growled as he rolled and grabbed her.

"Cold feet, warm heart, right?" Her giggling slowly turned to soft moans.

A bit later, Rusty sat on the side of the bed, lacing her boots.

"You and Dawson still planning to try and get over to Thompson today? It snowed again last night, I checked when I went down to get your birthday present. Looks like another inch at least. The horses aren't going to be happy with you at all."

"Those horses are getting fat. Standing around in the barn all day with the boy's filtching apples for them is beginning to show. I had trouble getting the saddle cinched up on Boss the other day. I thought he was holding his breath, but he's just bigger.

"Besides, one more inch of snow is just reason enough for us to get over to Thompson. We could really use another wood burning stove. If the stove that Frank remembers seeing at the general store is still there, it would help keep the house a lot warmer."

Griffin reached for Rusty and pulled her back down into the blankets, making her squeal.

"Now what's this about a birthday present?"

Thompson, before the EMP, had been a small but bustling rural town nestled in the valley between two mountains. The interstate had veered to the north in the 1950s, keeping Thompson's quiet individuality, if not an increased income.

As Griffin and Dawson rode into Thompson, Griffin looked around and saw that the town had finally changed. Empty and vandalized buildings bordered the street that ran through the village.

The EMP itself had challenged the inhabitants, but they had fallen back on the ways of their grandparents easily enough. Kerosene and wood replaced light bulbs and furnaces. Harness and bridle had been pulled from the barn attics. The preciously rare horses, mules and donkeys brought in from the field and wagons used as yard decorations had been repainted, repaired and put to use.

Life in many small, out-of-the –way towns in the Ozarks would have returned to the old ways if left to their own. Some towns, deep in the Ozark Mountains, had barely achieved twentieth-century living before the EMP. This in part, because the townsfolk had wanted it that way.

Thompson was not one of the lucky towns. Hoards from the cities had raced down this particular road and taken anything that had not been attached or nailed down.

The few that had tried to protect their belongings had either died or been chased away.

Griffin grabbed for the saddle horn as Boss crow-hopped when a plastic bag fluttered across the street in front of the horse. The horse pranced through the six inches of snow. Big, white puffs of air floated up as Boss snorted. He tossed his head, obviously enjoying the clear winter morning. The large gelding had practically leapt from the barn earlier that morning, having had his fill of his dark, boring stall.

Griffin leaned down and slapped a gloved hand on the frisky horse's neck. "That'll do, Boss." He growled, irritated the horse had caught him unaware. He shifted in the saddle, straightening back from the left sided slant that the horse had sent him into.

Griffin caught the multi-colored scarf as it tried to unwind from around his neck, lured by the icy wind, and threw it back around his neck and arm. The scarf, a present from Rusty, was soft and warm in the biting winter wind. Griffin smiled as he recalled the scene earlier that morning.

"Tobias has been teaching me how to knit. I know it's not perfect, I keep losing count and missing stitches, but I wanted to make you something special for your birthday." Rusty's cheeks glowed, in the soft light of early morning, from a mixture of pride and embarrassment.

"No, don't apologize." Griffin reached across the bed, inhaling the clean scent of Rusty's ebony hair, as he hugged her. "It is perfect. You put your heart into this and it means that much more to me because of it. Besides, it's pretty rocking. I mean, how many men will be out in this cold weather sporting a nice warm, neon green and pink scarf, huh? Hopefully not many, because I'd have to fight off all of them when they tried to take it. Then I might get it snagged on something, or…."

Rusty punched him lightly in the arm as she huffed in false annoyance. Before she could come back with some snarky remark though, Griffin swooped in and claimed her lips, kissing her thoroughly.

"I love it, thank you." He'd whispered and she had smiled and wrapped her arms around his neck, pulling him back down into the bed.

The dull impact of bullet to flesh, Boss shrieking even as he collapsed, Dawson shouting, "Ambush!", and the quiet town street mutated into a war zone, in a split second.

Griffin found himself flying through the air until he and the cracked asphalt connected in a jarring impact. Lying on the ground, staring up at the glacial blue sky, Griffin tried to breathe.

He had fallen off playground equipment as a child enough to know his breath would return, that it had only temporarily been knocked out of him, but that didn't stop the brief flare of panic in his chest.

His heartbeat thundered in his ears, blocking out any other noise around him. He rolled over to his side, seeing the broad back of Boss on the ground. Sound returned with his first breath. For a brief moment, he wished neither had.

Oxygen rushed into his lungs, burning. The scream of a mortally wounded horse all but blocked the sound of gunfire. Griffin crawled to the saddle, saying a prayer of thanks that Boss had fallen on his left side, leaving the rifle on the right of the saddle free.

Reaching up, sliding the rifle out of its sling in a smooth ark, the sun glinting off the barrel, he flicked the safety off. As Boss raised his massive head to let out another agonizing scream, Griffin put the barrel to the horse's head and pulled the trigger.

The rifle shot echoed in Griffin's own head, tears burned in his eyes even as he fought the bile back down his throat.

"Griff! You there, man?" Dawson shouted from behind a rusty Audi up the street. A bullet ricocheted off the bumper of the car, making Dawson twitch as he tried to make his body take up less space than it had since he was a baby.

"Yeah, I'm here Daws." Griffin, taking a peek up over the dead horse's back, he saw a rifle barrel poking out of the post office's broken front window. Sighting his own gun, he fired a round into the building's jagged opening.

A shocked shout proved that he had gotten their attention if nothing else. After a crash from inside the building, Griff could just make out voices. A heated argument led Griffin to believe that there were at least two people hiding just out of view of the window.

"Psst! Griff!" Dawson was violently indicating for Griffin to look up. Motioning with his fingers, he pointed to his own eyes, then up to the window in the second story of the building behind Griffin.

Griffin suddenly felt the hair rise on the back of his neck. Whipping around onto his back, his head and neck pushed up against the solid, cold leather of the saddle, he aimed his rifle up in the vicinity of Dawson's motions.

Seconds after he heard a sharp metal pop from the window to the right of his position in the street, a bullet slammed into the asphalt two inches from his right leg. He whipped the rifle up and sighted in the window and pulled the trigger before he had time to think of the movement.

A high pitched scream issued from the window just as a body toppled out of the opening. The old metal blinds screeched and popped, dragged through the window.

Griffin had instantly recognized the noise that had saved him. The popping sound of a metal blind being bent down for a person to peek through. A second later, the body and mess of tangled metal crashed to the sidewalk below the window.

A distraught yell from the post office had Griffin looking down the street to Dawson. The blonde giant still had the post office covered, so Griffin kept his own gun aimed at the window.

He heard the sound of scrambling feet. Shortly after, the sounds of horses neighing from behind the building then hoof beats receding from earshot.

He focused on the window above, waiting to see if anyone else was still up there. No sound after several minutes led him to believe that there had been only one, and he was now not a threat.

Cautiously, he and Dawson rose from behind horse and car. Griffin slowly walked over to the tangled mess on the sidewalk. Pulling the remains of the old blinds away from the body revealed a man not much older than Griffin. His greasy, rough-shorn brown hair and threadbare clothing showed just how hard life had recently been.

Dawson knelt down and felt for a pulse in the man's neck. Looking up at Griffin, he shook his head and stood up.

"Clean shot. Looks like it was right through the heart. Nothing you could have done different. It was you, me or him." Dawson scanned the area before sighing.

"Damn. One dead horse, the other's run off. We need transportation, Griff. If we can't find it, we may be stuck here for at least tonight. Let's go check out the post office. Maybe those bastards left something behind, besides their friend."

Dawson stood and began to walk away. Griffin tried to move, but couldn't. Looking down at the dead man, Griffin was vaguely aware of Dawson talking, but it seemed as if he were at one end of a tunnel. Dawson's voice had an echo-like quality. Griffin's vision seemed to be getting gray around the edge.

"Maybe we can catch my horse. It may have just run around the corner. I can see everyone back at the house freaking if it comes back without us…" Dawson turned as he spoke, and realized that Griffin was still back on the sidewalk.

"Shitdamnhell." Dawson turned and sprinted back to Griffin just as the other man began to crumble to the ground. Lunging at the last second, Dawson kept Griffin's head from smacking the concrete, hitting his own elbow on the hard surface instead.

"Son of a flying monkey's mother!" Dawson rubbed his throbbing elbow even as Griffin's eyes fluttered.

Griffin opened his eyes, confused that he was on the ground. Dawson's face suddenly loomed above.

"The first time you kill someone, it can just hit you out into left field. Happens. My first time, I puked so hard I thought my toes would come shooting out my mouth."

Dawson's calm matter-of-fact voice brought back what Griffin had done. Suddenly Griffin scrambled up on hands and knees to the curb, retching up breakfast. When he was done, he felt the other man's hand on his back.

"Let's go." Dawson calmly walked away.

Griffin had to work at it, but managed to pull himself together. Getting up, wiping his mouth on his coat sleeve, he picked up his rifle where it had clattered to the ground. One last glance at the dead man, and he stepped off the sidewalk and followed Dawson across the street.

Chapter eighteen

"Well, the fact that it's still hooked to the smokestack and able to heat this room comes in handy right now. I guess." Dawson grumbled, as he shoved wood into the small cast iron boxwood stove.

"Least it's still here." Griffin muttered, as he walked back into the building, holding an old copper kettle that he had just stuffed full of snow.

Stomping the snow off his boots, he walked over and set the kettle on one of the round cast iron disks on top of the age-blackened stove. "It won't hold much water, there's a crack in it half way up. Must be why it got tossed to begin with."

The ransacked general store had once been the central hub of the little community. Now, its empty shelves would provide warmth for the two men later that night as they fed planks into the wood burning stove. A thorough search hadn't yielded any food, leaving the men's stomachs growling in disgust. Fortunately, the huge pane of glass in the wooden frame at the front of the building remained unbroken, keeping the howling wind at bay.

The post office had yielded nothing but trash in the corners and spent rifle shell casings. Dawson had pocketed the shells. He had hopes of finding a re-loader one of these days.

The men worked through the building with no luck. Dawson, hand on the doorknob of the door leading out to the back alley, froze at the sound of movement on the other side of the exit. Both men cocked their rifles, one on either side of the door jam. Dawson lifted one, two then three fingers at Griffin. Turning the knob of the door, he quickly pushed the door away and out as he hugged the wall.

Silence greeted them. Then the rustling of bushes and a heavy thump of something on the ground. Griffin stuck his head out into the doorway and pulled it back quickly. Eyebrows pushed together in surprised confusion.

The mule, tied to a bare limbed elm tree, peeved at being left behind, gave a loud whinny-bray of frustration.

Both men slowly looked out the door to see a lonely mule, ready to make new friends.

"Huh, someone knotted the reins wrong. This one here," Dawson pointed to the mule, "must have jerked back at some time. Pulled the knot tighter. That's why they left you behind, huh." He reached up to scratch between the large rabbit-like ears of the mule. The mule nuzzled Dawson's chest, letting him know not to stop the scratching.

After fighting the knot for a few minutes, it was decided that they would have to cut the reins. The straps of leather would be short, but still functional.

The gain of transportation boosted their spirits and they went back to the main street and down the road to the small general store that had been the small town's version of Wal-Mart.

The store had been ransacked months ago, but both men were thankful that the stove and kettle had been left behind. Shortly after the men entered the abandoned building the weather had taken a turn.

Snow now blocked the view from the front glass window as a howling wind whipped the flakes past the building. The six inches of snow on the ground quickly became seven, then eight, with drifts climbing the walls of the buildings.

Griffin had managed to convince the mule to walk through the door into the, at least dry, building. It now lounged on three hooved legs over in the corner, nibbling at a sign that informed customers, "YOU BREAK IT; YOU BUY IT".

A quick search outside brought plenty of wood in for the duration of the storm, they hoped. Dawson had stripped saddle, saddlebags, bridle and reins from Griffin's horse. A small bag of dried apples and some beef jerky had been found in the saddlebags.

"I sure am glad Rusty looks after you so well, Griff. Remind me to give her a big ol' kiss when we get back." Dawson smiled as he dropped slivered beef jerky into the boiling water. The apple slices were already soaking in hot water in a small tin bowl on top of the stove.

"Tomorrow, we can rig up a sled of sorts for the stove. If we use a door for the sled, that and the rope we brought, hopefully will be enough to get the stove back to the farm." Dawson spoke as he fed wood into the hungry fire.

Griffin had been pulling needles off a pine branch, planning on making tea. It might not taste the best, but it would be better than drinking just hot water. He stopped working and looked up at the other man just as Dawson swore.

"The rope was with your horse."

"The rope is in my saddlebags. Son of a..." Both men spoke, drawing a bitter smile from Griffin.

Well, I guess we'll have to search up something else to use." Griffin shrugged his shoulder and continued de-needling the twig.

"Good idea, mixing the dried apples with the needle tea, Griff. Makes it a bit more palatable."

Griffin looked up from his own cup of tea.

"A bit more palatable? Who are you, Julia Child?"

Dawson smiled before he spoke.

"Huh, that just reminded me of a time when I was over in Iraq. I had pulled patrol duty one night with this other Marine. Now, I might be a big guy, but Tyrese Jones was a monster. Had to have been six nine if he stood an inch. Grew up in the back wood swamps of Louisiana. He said his great-great grandparents had been escaped slaves that holed up in the deep, dark bayous. Normally, his accent was so thick, you had to really concentrate on what he said, ya know? Used to drive our C.O. crazy, cuz he'd have to get another kid from Louisiana to translate for'm.

"Anyway, Tyrese loved to quote Shakespeare. First time I heard him, we was walking through camp, ya know, a whole group of us, headed for the showers. I just stopped walking, stood there like an idiot. I think my jaw was touching the ground."

Dawson laughed at the memory.

"I think he did it on purpose. He made it to the showers before all of us. Got the last of the hot water."

"I don't get it, Daws. So he could quote the Bard. Hell, I know "To be, or not to be: that is the question." I had to read *Romeo and Juliet* in high school."

"Uh, that's from *Hamlet*." Dawson snickered.

"Whatever, man. My point is, even I can quote the man. What's the big deal?"

"The thing was, when he got to quoting, it was usually *Macbeth* by the way, his thick southern accent vanished and I swear, he turned British or something."

"Really?" Griffin looked and sounded skeptical.

"I mean it! He just changed! And it wasn't just his voice, it was his entire bearing. He stood straighter; he was elegant! He would flow when he moved. With that and his change in enunciation, you'd have thought he had studied Shakespeare at Oxford. I tell ya, it was spooky.

"So that night, we had pulled the night patrol on the eastern perimeter of camp. It was one of those creepy, still nights that Iraq has a lot of.

"Now, the Bedouins believe that is a man dies of thirst in the desert, he turns into a green owl and flies over the desert dunes for a thousand years, screaming for water. It was *that* kind of creepy night.

"Me and Tyrese are walking the perimeter and he's going all Macbeth on me. He had just finished quoting Lady Macbeth. You know "Out, damned spot! Out, I say!", when we hear this scream out in the dunes. The hair on my arms jumped up to attention. I still get chills thinking about it.

"We both stopped dead in our tracks, trying to pinpoint where in the dunes we'd heard it, and it floats out over the sand again. I was starting to freak, hell, so was Tyrese. When all of a sudden this big-ass bird comes swooping over us. We see it soar up above us and then really slow like it turned and dove down. It kept screaming over and over, and we just stood there like statues. When I think back, I don't think I could have moved, it was like we were in some kind of trance. I felt its wings brush my face. I thought for a second it was going for me, but at the last second it changed its course. Next thing I knew, it was on Tyrese. He screamed once, He had dropped his rifle when the bird hit, his hands were up trying to pull the thing off his face.

"Then he just dropped, Tyrese I mean. The second his body started to fall the bird lifted up off'm. It screamed one more time as it flew off and then it was past a dune and I never heard it again."

Griffin waited. Dawson was staring off into space, reliving that night. Griffin could almost see the terror in the other man's eyes. Or maybe it was just the darkening shadows creeping in on them from the corners of the room.

"So, was it the green owl? Did Tyrese die?" Griffin asked in a whisper. Goose bumps crawled up and down his arms. The wind howling outside in the now-dark street, lent to the creepy atmosphere.

"Naw, just some hawk that didn't like Shakespeare." Dawson grinned and stood to shove more wood in the stove.

Griffin sat and stared at his friend, blank faced.

"What?" Blankness was pushed over by confusion.

Dawson burst out laughing. "It was a night hawk, dude! Just looking for a meal. Must have figured Tyrese looked like a giant mouse or something. It scratched the hell out'a his helmet. And Tyrese fainted. I'll bet he will never forget that night."

He walked back over and pushed Griffin's mouth shut.

"Better try and get some shut eye, my friend, long day tomorrow." Dawson went over to one of the piles of pine boughs and lay down, smiling.

It suddenly clicked with Griffin that he had been duped.

"You ass! You just made that all up! I feel like an idiot, thanks a lot!"

"What's in a name? That which we call a rose by any other name would smell as sweet..." Dawson rolled over in his make shift bed, still chortling as he did.

Chapter nineteen

"Rusty, come away from that window. All you're doing is fogging it up, and it won't stop the snow anyways." Drew stirred the huge pot of stew another turn then poured two cups of hot coffee and motioned for Rusty to join him at the scarred work table.

A large pine log sparked and popped in the fireplace. Warmth pushed out into the large kitchen. Kerosene lanterns hung from the ceiling above the table, flames creating a flickering light show.

The entire room reminded Rusty of a Currier and Ives painting on a serving tray her grandmother had had when Rusty visited her ten years ago. She remembered thinking then that the scene looked so warm and inviting. Now, as she wrapped her sweater around herself tighter as a frigid draft seeped in from the window, she didn't feel warm and invited at all.

Griffin and Dawson should have been back to the farm last evening. Dusk and the coming snow storm had brought only Dawson's horse galloping into the barn just ahead of the blowing blizzard that still raged outside.

Rusty sat at the table and stirred a spoonful of honey into her coffee. She began to say again how worried she was, then figuratively popped herself on the back of her head. She was worried, but so was every other member on the farmstead. Saying it again, wasn't going to do anything but frustrate her and the others.

Colleen, Susan and Josh had tried to ride out earlier, when the morning sun had risen but failed to break through the storms fury. Within an hour of leaving, they had returned nearly frozen.

"They could have been ten feet away from us and we'd of never seen them in passing." Colleen had brought the hot mug of beef broth to her mouth after she spoke.

Susan nodded, forgoing speech to keep her teeth from chattering.

"I wager they're hold up somewhere, waiting for the storm to blow itself out. Whatever trouble they ran into that caused them to lose the horse is the least of their worries right now." Josh spoke soft, aware of Rusty's worry. He'd looked her square in the eye as he spoke again.

"Those two boys have their heads on straight. They'll do what needs to be done to stay alive. Worrying doesn't do anything but cause ulcers."

Now, in the early afternoon, Rusty could hear the kids in the living room. The Monopoly game have been going on for two hours now. Missy had brought it down from her room and rounded up the three boys to play. After the first hour spent teaching Zane how to play the board game, Missy had proceeded to buy up all the real estate and charge the boys rent every time they landed on her property. Joey was currently wailing.

"I don't have any more money to pay you Miss!"

"I'll pay your rent for you Joey. Here, is this enough?" Zane kindly offered.

"Whahoo! I get to use my "Get Out Of Jail" card finally! Maybe I should stay one night though, just so's I can say I did. Ya think?" Thomas chattered excitedly.

Missy bought up Park Place and gloated when Zane landed on it, "That's two hundred dollars, Zane."

"Uh, hey Joey, can I borrow some of your money?" Zane asked anxiously.

Rusty smiled in spite of the worry. At least the kids had the game, taking their minds off of the storm and the two missing men.

Drew brought Rusty's attention back into the kitchen when he softly laid his callused hand over hers.

"They will be alright." He smiled at her as he spoke.

Rusty turned her hand to squeeze Drew's, smiled back and nodded. "Thanks Drew."

Taking in a deep breath and sitting up straighter, she began, "You know, Josh said something the other day. We need a historian. You know, someone to write down our journeys. All of us here at the farm. How we got here, to this point. We have a story that shouldn't be forgotten. We are a part of this huge world changing event, this stupid EMP. I'm going to take it on. In fact, I'm going to start right now. I'm going to go find paper and pencil, don't go away, I want your life story when I get back."

She jumped up to go, turned back and hugged Drew and whispered in his ear. "Thanks Drew."

Drew continued to sip his hot coffee, a smile on his face as Rusty raced through the house, tracking down the essentials needed to record what he considered a very lackluster life of a farmer. Maybe he could spice it up a bit, after all, it might end up in a history book someday.

The braying mule woke the men with a start. The first thing Griffin noticed was the silence outside. The second was the decidedly barn-like odor of the general store.

Dawson yawned and ran his hands across his blonde crew cut.

"Storms finally blown itself out. Let's go out and see what it's left us. Mule definitely needs to go outside." He walked over and tried to look out the glass door.

The storm outside and the heat inside had fought each other, leaving a thick opaque frost on the glass panel.

Pulling the door open, Dawson kicked through the snow drift that had settled in the doorway.

Griffin followed with the mule on his heels, breathing on his neck.

The men squinted, Dawson shading his eyes with his hand. The storm had roared and torn across the land for a full two days, keeping man and beast trapped in the building.

Now the morning sun rose over the almost pristine landscape. A set of rabbit tracks wound from behind the building and down the street, but nothing living had been out of its burrow, den or shelter until now. Trees shimmered with ice and snow. A crow swooped down in the sky to land on the roof of the building across from the men, berating them with several "caws" before flapping its wings and soaring off to the east.

The three stood knee-deep in snow, silently taking in the drifts and depths of the snow. A mountain of snow on the north side of "Henrietta's Hair Palace" reached to the roof of the building. Smaller drifts could be seen up and down the street.

"I'll bet we got a good six, seven more inches from this one. It's gonna be a bitch getting home. How about we do a quick look-see and try and find something that would work as a sled and hopefully some rope? Otherwise, we'll have to head back without the stove." Dawson clapped his hands together, startling the mule, who jerked its head up and brayed loudly.

Griffin, reins in hand, tightened his grip. "Don't get any ideas, Borax, we don't need you running off."

"Borax? Isn't that some kind of laundry soap?" Dawson laughed and began trudging through the snow to the next building.

Griffin followed, Borax nudging him every step of the way.

"Yeah, mom always used it when I was growing up. I remember the box it came in showed this wagon with a long string of mules pulling it. So, now I think of that when I see a mule. He needs a name, if he had one, we don't know it, so…"

"Guess that's as good as any." Dawson replied. "Bring Borax into the building with us. Can't afford to lose him." With that, he pushed the door of the beauty salon and went in.

"I want to go out with you Josh."

"I know you do Rusty. I was going to catch you before you headed out to tend livestock, as a matter of fact. Susan's under the weather this morning."

"Is she alright?" Rusty was instantly worried for her friend.

"Oh sure, head cold is all. I've got her tucked in on the couch in the surgery room with eucalyptus oil simmering on the stove. She's grumbling about being pampered, so she's not feeling too rough.

"That's why I wanted to talk with you. I'd like for you and Colleen to go out with me to look for Griff and Dawson. I don't suppose I'll have to twist your arm, will I? Dress warm and…"

Josh stopped talking. Rusty was off at a run up the back staircase.

"Thank God you're taking her out with you today, Doc. She near exhausted me yesterday with all of her questions about myself. I know it kept her mind busy and all, but she is damn nosy! Can put those tabloid reporters to shame." Drew had walked into the kitchen for coffee as Rusty galloped through the house.

"She has a little terrier in her for sure. She'll worry something fierce until she has it all worked out in her head." Tobias ambled out of the pantry with a canister of dried oats.

Josh smiled at Tobias, "Consider yourself saved for a day or two. She told me last night she was moving from Drew to you, Tobias. Best be thinking up something to make your life sound a little intriguing.

The older man slammed the metal jar down on the counter, a scowl on his craggy face. "I'll wager my life has had more "intrigue" than either of you pups could ever have dreamed up. Still, it's a good thing to get Rusty out of the house. She's likely to gnaw off her own foot to get free afore too much longer."

"Well that's just a disgusting analogy Tobias. I love you too." Rusty strolled through the kitchen door, dressed in woolen sweater, socks pulled over jeans tucked into jeans and a thick knitted cap on her head. A coat was draped over her arm. She laughed as she added, "Your probably right though, another day and I would be bouncing off the walls.

"I passed Kevin on the stairs, he wants to go too. Do you mind Josh?" Rusty, her best soulful puppy dog eyes directed at the retired military doctor.

"I don't like leaving the farm with so few armed adults. But I suppose if Tobias can manage to scrape the rust off his joints, he can keep the youngsters in line should something come up. There shouldn't be much moving around out there today."

"Well now, I just might manage to move my crotchety old bones enough to keep the wolves at bay. Now, git on with ya. I've got oatmeal cookies to bake. Go find those boys."

Rusty hugged the old man, saying a quick prayer under her breath that they did indeed find Griffin and Dawson. Then she was out the door, headed to the barn to start saddling the horses.

Josh stuck his head up the stairwell, "Let's go Kevin! We leave in ten."

Before leaving the house, Josh stopped by the surgery. Susan was standing by the window, watching as Rusty led two saddled horses out of the barn, followed by Kevin and Colleen with their own mounts plus an extra horse.

"You should be resting and under a quilt." Josh came up behind Susan and wrapped his arms around her.

Susan brought her hands up to hold his. "Be careful out there Josh. I'll worry until I see all of you riding back in through the front gates. Do you think it's a good idea for Rusty to go? If something has happened…"

"Let's not think the worst yet. Rusty needs to go, you know that. I'm doing you a favor, she would be in here driving you nuts. She needs to stay busy, this will do it."

Susan sniffed as she turned in his arms. She kissed his cheek, "I don't want you to catch this cold. Go."

"Maybe should have thought about that last night, eh?" Josh grinned as he reciprocated, planting a chaste kiss on her forehead.

Susan watched the group mount up and ride out of the yard, "Bring them all home, God. Please." She wondered briefly if God was even still listening, before going to the couch, curling up under the quilt, and closing her eyes.

Rusty would have enjoyed the cold ride if not for the worry. The landscape glistened with blinding white snow. Tiny birds had fluffed snow off of their feathers to flitter in small groups looking for seeds. A bush the group rode by had tiny red berries peeking out from underneath clumps of snow, invited the creatures to wake and feast.

They followed the road that led into to Thompson. A few drifts needed to be skirted, but the wind had kept the flat road fairly clear except where the hills rose up with the ribbon of road between them. In these spots, the riders dismounted, leading the horses. Plowing through the snow with their bodies was cold and slow work. Better though than having a horse break a leg. Rocks fell from the hills with regularity. In the past, road crews removed the hazards. Those days had passed.

As they rounded a curve in the road, the group checked their weapons. No sign of the missing men during the ride had made the group edgy. The town of Thompson came into view.

"We knew we'd see nothing after the storm, any tracks out here were swept away." Colleen commented as they rode.

There was a quiet hush over the town as the group rode in. Josh reined in his horse as they neared the post office. An enormous mound of snow blocked part of the road. The group stopped and Josh dismounted. As he slowly walked over to the snow dune, the others readied their rifles.

Squatting down, he brushed a patch of snow off.

Rusty gasped when she saw the white patch of hair on the right shoulder of the dead horse.

"It's Boss." Her voice quavered as she spoke.

"Doc." Kevin pointed with his chin to a smaller mound next to a building.

Rusty jumped from her horse and lunged through the drifted snow. She fell on her knees and began to push snow from the pile.

Kevin and Colleen, rifles in hand dismounted and followed.

Rusty brushed the snow from the head. Tears sprang to her eyes, a soft sob escaped her.

"It's not him. It's not Griffin."

Kevin came and lifted her up, hugging her.

Rusty struggled to control her emotions. The dead man was not Griffin or Dawson, the relief she felt barely topped the guilt that surged through her. This man was dead…but Griffin wasn't. She repeated the mantra "Griffin wasn't" in her head over and over.

"It was an ambush." Josh stood, brushed the snow from his jeans. He pointed down to the horse, "He took a bullet to the shoulder. He was down. Came from there." He pointed to the abandoned post office.

"But this one," he pointed over to the dead man, "he was up there I'd wager." He nodded to the broken window up above the group.

"We have to find them." Rusty broke from Kevin and strode over to her horse and mounted, followed by the others. Before she could rein her horse over past Boss though, Josh grabbed the horse's bridle. The horse jerked its head, but remained still.

"We'll go. But we'll go as a group, and we'll go smart."

Rusty drew in a deep breath and nodded. "You're right. I just…"

"I know." Josh reached out and squeezed her knee.

Josh had just hit the saddle when a loud braying erupted from behind the buildings to the left. The raucous sound continued, followed by an irritated voice. Unable to understand the words, the voice though left no doubt as to who was scolding the braying mule.

"Dawson." Kevin smiled out the word. They all broke into a canter, down the street, around the corner and face to face with the welcoming committee.

Borax was overjoyed to see hooved friends. He brayed one longer strung out hello before Dawson grabbed the mules lip and tugged hard.

"Borax, if you don't shut up, we may eat you, I am very hungry!" The noise of the other horses coming down the street had Dawson raising his rifle. In the next moment he lowered it and called out, "Wondered when you'd show up! Can't say I'm not glad to see ya either!"

Hearing the ruckus from the mule, Griffin came barreling out of the small automotive store, tow rope in one hand, rifle in the other.

"Griff!" Rusty kicked her horse into a trot, then leapt from the saddle to hug Griffin, kissing him deeply. He dropped the tow rope and encircled her with one arm.

After several seconds, Dawson cleared his throat and coughed.

"I think there's a hotel of sorts down the street. Just sayin'."

Laughter followed as the riders all dismounted and Dawson explained the events of the past two days.

"Luckily we were able to pull a shelf away from a wall at the general store, and it looks like Griff lucked out on the rope. I can't believe it got left behind."

"I know! I think it must have been forgotten at one time or another, it was stashed up on a top shelf, way back in a corner, probably been there for a decade." Griffin had finally come up for air, grinning.

"The stove should be cool enough to take apart by now. Let's get on over to the general store and pull it down. I don't suppose ya'll brought any food with ya? I wasn't kidding when I told this fool mule I'd eat him." Dawson tugged Borax's mane as he spoke. Borax vocalized his feelings and nudged the man's chest.

The group began walking back over to the old grocery store. Griffin and Rusty lagged behind the rest. Rusty reached over and grasped Griffin's hand.

"When I saw Boss…" Rusty's voice broke and she gripped Griffin's hand tighter.

"I know. Listen, I know you were worried and I wish, God I wish none of this had happened. It did though. The thing is, right now I can't talk about it. If you really need to know, Daws can tell you, but right now, here, I just can't." Griffin had stopped walking, turned to face Rusty.

Rusty looked into his eyes and knew he was in a bad way. Torment, sorrow and …guilt?

She reached up and gently touched his cheek and smiled.

"You'll tell me when you're ready. Just remember, I'll always be here for you. I love you."

He released her hand and engulfed her in a hug. She could feel him trembling as she hugged him back. He tightened his hold, a ragged sob slipped out.

Rusty felt tears threaten to spill but forced them back. Griffin needed her strength now and her crying wouldn't help. It broke her heart that he was hurting like this. He had always been the strong one. Since day one of this new world, he had been the one that kept her spirits up as they traveled into Kansas to get Kevin. It was Griffin that had laughed after he tried flipping light switches on in an abandoned gas station the night before they had met Josh on the outskirts of Wichita.

Griffin had changed since they had lain in bed, laughing at her lack of ability to knit. Had it really only been a few days ago that they had been so light hearted?

A deep breath and Griffin pulled back, quickly wiping his eyes and sniffing. He smiled. It was tremulous, but it was a smile and Rusty would take it and be happy with it.

They started walking again, holding hands, in silence.

Chapter twenty

Spring arrived in the Ozarks in an array of greens. The hills, covered in bare, sleeping trees were suddenly tinted with hints of white, pink and neon green. Purple Grape Hyacinth burst out of snowdrifts on the east side of the house. Daffodils, Iris, and Tulips followed and soon the front yard was a palette of color.

Dandelions were quickly picked by the children and Zane. The bitter taste of the greens from the yellow flower were a pleasant change from winter fare. Jelly and salve from the prolific weed soon stocked the kitchen pantry and the surgery's shelves.

The stove that had been brought home from Thompson graced the front sitting room where Griffin and Rusty had spent the cold evenings. Rusty continued to document life stories from all the residents of the farm. Even the animals had chapters, since Zane had declared their stories important as well.

"Did you know that Gracie the goat doesn't like women? Zane said she told him that shortly after he took over the milking. She said that women have cold hands." Rusty looked up from her stack of papers that grew taller as the days passed.

"And Borax told him that you were the best thing to ever happened to him. Guess we know who rates with the livestock around here."

Griffin looked up from a page in a book he had been staring at for the last twenty minutes. "Well, you do have cold hands, and obviously I'm a God in the equine realm. Truth hurts, Babe." He dodged the eraser lobbed at his head and got up to walk over and wrap his arms around Rusty.

"I like your cold hands, you're better than any alarm clock my mom ever tried on me. Who cares what a crazy goat thinks anyway?"

"You had that nightmare again last night. Do you want to talk about it?" Rusty pulled Griffin around to sit at the table beside her.

For the last two months, since the trip to Thompson, Griffin cried out in his sleep several times a week.

Rusty had talked to Josh and Dawson and knew what had gone down in the small town. She had privately wept for the Griffin she had lost that day. The man who had never dreamt that he would ever be forced to take a life in order to save his own. He was a changed man now. One that wasn't as fast with a laugh as he once had been. One that sought out moments of solitude where before he needed other people.

Griffin looked away from Rusty, swallowing hard, he shook his head. "I…I don't ever remember them. I don't want to either." He stood and walked to the window, hands in the pockets of his jeans.

Rusty followed and wrapped her arms around his waist. They stood for a time, only the sound of birds outside broke the silence.

"Boss screamed. When they shot him. He wouldn't stop. He just screamed over and over, until I shot him. My ears where ringing from the screaming and the rifle shot. The silence was almost painful, ya know?

"Then Dawson motioned behind me. And...before I even thought about what I was doing I was rolling onto my back and was shooting. Maybe he was just watching. Maybe he was never gonna shoot. I can see him. Dead on the sidewalk. He might have had a family, someone waiting for him."

She could feel his the tremors racing through his body, reliving the memories of that day. She kissed his back and spoke quietly.

"You saved yourself and Dawson. You know, deep down, you know that they wouldn't have let you walk away. You did what needed to be done. I hate that you had no choice. I hate that it was forced on you like that. But, I'm glad you did it. Because I don't think I could be standing here today if you hadn't come back, Griff. When that horse came back alone, I thought the worst. Turns out it was almost the worst.

"You're still a good person Griffin. If you didn't feel guilty, you would be as bad as those that tried to hurt you. Your guilt is your humanity."

Griffin turned in her arms, wrapping her in his. His eyes were red and full of unshed tears. He kissed her, "I love you Rusty."

"I love you too. Now, how about we go out and ride? It's a gorgeous spring day, I hear there are baby calves out in the north pasture, and there is a mule out in the barn that would love to carry his idol through a couple pastures."

Griffin rolled his eyes at the thought of Borax and his beliefs but smiled down at Rusty and nodded.

"Well congratulations Ben, you've got chicken pox. Mrs. McClelland, he's contagious as long as he has the fever. It's probably too late now for quarantine. I'm sure he and his brothers and sisters have all been in close quarters of each other. Don't scratch Ben.

"Susan, let's try some of that dandelion salve that Tobias make up last week and write the recipe down for Mrs. McClelland here. If it works on Ben, I'm sure she'll need more soon."

Josh took the seven year olds hand away from his neck. The red head had freckles on top of freckles. The red spots from the chicken pox were camouflaged amongst all the other dots.

Susan, reached for the small jar of golden ointment on the shelf by the window, glancing out.

"Looks like Tobias had better start a new batch for us too."

Josh and Ben's mother came over and looked out into the barnyard. There they saw Joey, Thomas and Zane playing with the other two McClelland boys.

"Oh no!" Exclaimed Mrs. McClelland.

"I should have left those two home with their father! It never even crossed my mind that this rash was contagious! My husband and I honestly thought this was some sort of reaction to my first try at making lye soap. I am so sorry…"

Josh shook his head and waved a hand to dismiss the guilt-filled woman's speech.

"It's a normal part of childhood. Best to get it out of the way now in the spring. Summers too hot with the fever thrown into it, winter requires too many clothes on top of fever and itch. Don't worry about those boys, they'll bounce back quickly if they catch it."

Ushering the woman and her scratching son out the door, Josh walked back to the window and looked out again.

The four boys and Zane were playing leap frog. The boys, all shrieking and laughing in delight as each one managed to leap over Zane's back. After rolling into a cushion of hay they would jump up and run to get in line to do it again.

A call from the house brought an end to the game. Goodbyes were made, and two of the boys skipped off to meet their mother and sibling in the front yard.

"You look worried. I thought you told Gladys not to worry about the kids catching it?" Susan stepped back in the room, to disinfect the examination table.

"Hmm? Oh, it's not the kids I'm worried about. It's Zane. Do you know if he had them as a boy? He's still young enough it may not be a worry if he does get them." He turned and watched Susan spray the table before wiping the alcohol away with a clean towel.

"Chicken pox in adults can be more serious. Inflammation of joints, some organs…heart, liver, kidneys. Blood clots can be a major risk factor, especially now with no way to get our hands on anti-clotting meds. Let's just keep an eye on all of them. Tobias should stay clear too, come to think of it. If he had the chicken pox as a child he's still carrying the virus. Put's him at risk for shingles. I'm sure he wouldn't want to deal with that."

"I'm definitely sure *I* don't want Tobias getting shingles!" Susan said with a grin. "That man can be positively evil when his arthritis acts up; can you imagine what he would be like with a painful rash like shingles?"

"You're right. Let's keep the boys, all of the boys out of the kitchen for the next week, just to be safe." Josh chuckled.

The soft thud of hooves on thick pasture grass and the creaking of saddle leather merged magically with the birdsong. The wind whispered through tree branches thick with buds, flowers and tiny green leaves. A squirrel paused on its journey to scold the riders as they passed under the small rodent.

Rusty drew the warm spring air greedily into her lungs and laughed when an explosive sneeze from Griffin paused the squirrel's chattering.

"Ten years of allergy shots and I still do this every spring! Where's the justice?" Griffin sniffed and sneezed once more.

"You should try some of the tea that Drew was brewing for Missy this morning. It's his grandmother's go- to for spring allergies."

"Yeah well, that "go to" smells like the hyena exhibit two hours after feeding time. I think I can live with a few sneezy moments."

Rusty laughed at the memory. "Those poor animals always smelled! It wasn't just after feeding. Oh, look!" She slowed her horse and pointed to the left.

Griffin nudged Borax closer to Rusty's horse. The trees opened up to the big north valley pasture. The meadow, yellow and snow covered most of the winter, now was a crisp spring green with a patchwork of flowers scattered here and there.

"Six, no seven calves! Look at them Griff! Aren't baby animals just the most adorable things ever created? Let's see if we can get a little closer." She nudged her horse to move on.

"Let's not get too close. It only makes the mamas nervous. Here, I snagged the binoculars from the house. Use them and you can check out the calves." Griffin moved up beside Rusty, turned sideways, searching in the saddlebag for the glasses. Pulling them out, he handed them over with a smile.

"Thanks, baby." Rusty smiled sweetly as she took the glasses. Turning her horse back into the shade of the trees, she watched the cattle grazing.

Griffin listened as Rusty gave running commentary on every single cow and calf in the field, but kept his own eyes scanning over the meadow and on up the oval shaped top of the valley. The recent ambush was still on his mind, and he had no intention of riding into another any time soon.

Trees lined the top of the valley completely. Pioneers and farmers had cleared the trees in the basin; making it a grassy meadow for livestock, but the forest remained on alert, ready to reclaim its place on the land. Griffin even now, could see saplings growing on the upper slopes of the valley. Clusters of blackberry and gooseberry bushes dotted the basin, thick with blooms. He would have to remember to check them out in the late summer and see if the cattle and wildlife had left any fruit that could be picked and made into preserves and pies.

Sun glinting off metal drew his eyes to the farthest lip of the valley. Reacting instantly, he jumped off the mule as he pulled Rusty from her horse. Before Rusty could raise a fuss or question Griffin's actions a rifle shot echoed across the land.

"There's someone with a gun over on the far side. We need to get our horses back into the trees, now." Griffin barked. Rusty had the good sense for once to follow orders without balking.

Back in the dark shadows of the newly leafed trees, Griffin watched the far tree line.

Rusty gasped, "One of the cows is down!" She pointed down into the meadow just as a rifle shot sounded once more. Another cow dropped. The herd scattered now, thoroughly spooked by the smell of blood from two of its members. One calf remained by the side of its mother, bawling in confusion, then it suddenly dropped, too, with the sound of gunfire.

"My god, they're slaughtering the herd!" Griffin swore as he turned and slid his rifle from its scabbard on the saddle.

"Rusty, take the horses further back into the trees, I don't want you or them getting hit."

"What are you doing?" Rusty asked as Griffin stepped over to a large rock and squatted behind it, rifle resting on the top of it.

"I'm going to stop them from killing any more of our cattle, now go!" At that, he aimed over at where he had seen the flash of metal, and fired a shot.

Rusty grabbed the mule's reins along with her horse's and turned them back into the trees calling over her shoulder,

"Get those sons of bitches, but keep your head down!"

Griffin smiled grimly. That was his Rusty. Pissed when someone hurt hers, but always with a little common sense thrown in.

Another cow had been dropped but the shooting stopped when Griffin fired back. The herd was running away, towards the east fence line. Griffin hoped that that corner of the field was out of rifle range from where the original shot had occurred.

Just as he was wishing he had grabbed the binoculars from Rusty, something moved on his left.

Rusty was standing behind a large elm tree, binoculars up to her eyes.

"Jeez Rusty! I never even heard you come back! Where are the horses? I thought I told you to get safe." Griffin grumbled.

"I used my ninja-like skills. The horses are safe, stop worrying. Did you think I was gonna let you have all the fun kicking ass?" She smiled as she spoke, still scanning through the lenses. Looking over at him she turned to face him, showing her right hand. Her rifle that she had fought so hard not to have to touch was gripped tightly.

Having given into the fact that she had to learn to shoot, she had made herself practice until she was as good as Coleen and Josh.

"I see movement! Look to the left of that tall cottonwood with the broken limb hanging." Handing the lenses to Griffin, she tried using her scope on her rifle to see the men in the trees.

"There are at least three of them. Careful, one is looking for us. I see him looking through his scope."

"I see him. Yeah, I see two others, too. Watch it! He's looking right at us!" Griffin ducked down below the rock as he spoke.

A shot rang across the valley, a bullet hitting a tree ten feet left of them. Rusty inched out just enough from behind her tree to use her scope again.

Griffin hissed, "Rusty! Get back!"

Rusty remained where she was, "He's guessing. That shot was too far off us. If he had seen us, that shot would have been closer."

"Maybe he's just a sucky shot. Now get behind that tree!" Exasperated, Griffin was motioning for her to move.

"He shot those cows one bullet per cow, he doesn't suck. There you are, you ass. Now don't move..."

Griffin jerked when Rusty's rifle barked. He raised enough to use the binoculars again. There was a flurry of movement across the valley. One man was getting up from the ground. He bent down to pick up something. Looking at the object, a look of utter rage flooded the man's face.

The man looked up and across the span and looked directly into Griffin's eyes. Griffin knew that the man couldn't really see him at that distance; still he jerked the binoculars down and scrambled back.

"What did you do Rusty? We need to get out of here, you really pissed them off."

Rusty turned with a satisfied grin on her face.

"I shot the scope of his rifle. He won't be shooting anymore cattle with it."

A bullet ripped into the tree Rusty was standing behind, causing a girl-like squeal to pop out of her, much to her embarrassment.

"Uh, yeah, we should go." She duck walked over to Griffin and they proceeded to crawl farther back into the trees before running to their mounts and racing back to the house.

Chapter twenty one

"How many were out there?" Josh asked the couple.

Rusty and Griffin had raced back to the farmstead where an emergency meeting was called. It was there, in the massive kitchen that all the residents of Fort Repose gathered. The boys where asking questions one after another, not waiting for answers, while the adults murmured after hearing of the shootings.

It was Josh's question, issued in a no-nonsense, commanding voice that stopped the others. He sat at the head of the table, drawing the attention of the other adults, some sitting, some standing. It was Rusty, pacing the room, still too full of adrenaline to sit, that answered.

"I saw the one with the rifle, it had huge scope too. There were two others that I saw. Both men, I was focused on the creep with the rifle though. I don't know what weapons they had. They all looked pretty scruffy though. Long, greasy hair, just nasty looking."

"So, at least three." Josh contemplated for a moment before continuing, "We need to go bring in the remaining cattle, we can't afford to lose any more food. There's going to be plenty of predators out there come nightfall. If we ride around the hill that you and Rusty were on.." He looked to Griffin, "we can get to the south gate without putting ourselves up on a horizon. We send one in to scope out the pasture. We don't want a fire fight out there if we can avoid it. We round up the remaining herd and haul ass home. We can put the cows and calves in the field behind the barn for a couple of weeks."

"We don't have to worry about the scope on that rifle. Rusty blew it away. You said she was improving, but damn, Josh, you didn't say she was sniper material!" Griffin grinned at Rusty as he spoke.

She felt her cheeks heat up at the compliment. She had practiced hard when she had been forced to pick up a gun. Oddly enough, as much as she had been loath to handle a weapon, she was a natural. The rifle became an extension of her body when she was shooting.

"I could understand shooting a cow, hunger is a pretty big incentive, but they were shooting the calves too! From what I saw through my scope, they were enjoying it way too much. They weren't hunting, they were playing. I'm glad he won't be using that scope again, maybe even the rifle."

"Whoever they are, we've made an enemy so we need to all be alert. Dawson, you and Kevin, Frank and myself..." Josh was interrupted before finishing, as Colleen spoke up.

"Josh, we need you here. You're our doctor. Not only do we need you healthy and whole, the outlying farms do too." Colleen stood as she spoke, looking towards the others for assurance.

Drew nodded as he voiced his opinion, "Colleen's right. You're our leader, I'm sure everyone would agree to that, but you are also our healer, and that's a pretty darned important job. I'll ride out with the boys. I've at least herded before so I won't be a third wheel."

Before Josh could nix the idea, the rest of the group firmly agreed, reminding him that they worked as a democracy, not a dictatorship.

"Fine, but I want all of you on red alert the entire time, understood? We could have some major conflict because of this incident. Go get the cattle and get back here before nightfall."

The group broke up. Some, going to saddle horses, some to check the weapon's supply. There wasn't a huge choice of weapons, but all were common, and all had plenty of ammunition. Many of Josh patients paid in ammo along with garden produce or jobs done for the farm.

When the four rode out of the barnyard, several silent prayers went out for safe return of men and beasts.

The setting sun was vivid just above the treetops when the bellows of upset bovine came floating into the windows of the house. The three boys whooped and hollered as the cattle came up the outside of the pasture by the barn. Zane ran over to the gate and opened it, calling the cows in by shaking a bucket of grain to bribe them to enter the field.

All four riders where dusty, but grinning as the last of the cows followed Zane.

"I swear, Zane is a piper and those cows are mice. He has the magic touch with every animal I've seen him with," Rusty spoke softly to Josh as they watched the riders gather in the barnyard.

"He has something akin to magic, for sure," Josh smiled as he replied then walked over towards the riders.

Kevin rode into the pasture along with the cattle. A lone cow circled around the rest of the herd and bellowed belligerently at Kevin. Kevin, calf in front of him in the saddle, hefted the little creature up and swung his leg over the neck of his grazing horse. Sliding down to the ground he set the small calf down as it issued a baby bellow of its own. It wobbly made its way over to the fretful mother who proceeded to lick the baby and shoot Kevin with an evil bovine glare. The calf soon found its mothers udder and stopped complaining.

Kevin led his horse back through the gate, "She had just given birth a little bit before we got there! Drew said it was probably stress induced, but I think he is going to make it. He and his momma bawled at each other the entire trip."

"He is adorable, Kevin!" Rusty smiled as she hugged her brother, relief at seeing him safe, surging along with happiness at seeing the baby.

"Any sign of trouble?" Josh asked as the Dawson walked up. Dawson shook his head in disgust.

"Coyotes where already on the carcasses, so I'm gonna guess the sons-a-bitches were gone. The cattle were easy, they wanted out of the area pretty damn bad." Drew said as he walked up.

As Drew joined the group he was more than a bit nostalgic as he watched Coleen and Frank hug and quietly talk to each other. Drew's own wife, Patty, had been taken from him seven years ago from cancer. He still missed her fiercely, and while he would never begrudge his friends their love for each other, at times it reminded him of his own loss.

"Good news that." Josh clasped Drew's shoulder. He had seen the emotions, fleetingly, in Drew's eyes, as Frank crossed over to Colleen. Maybe he would bring the topic up with Susan later. He seemed to recall a certain Irish lady that blushed prettily at every encounter with the farmer.

Tobias appeared in the kitchen window, approval at seeing the livestock safe and sound along with all of his adopted family, and bellowed out, "Supper's not getting any hotter, but it sure as shootin' will get colder if'n ya don't hightail it inside, all of ya!" The crankiness of voice was downsized by the immense grin spread across his face.

The boys, always hungry, yelled happily and all ran for the house.

"Boys, make sure you wash up first." Colleen called out to the two boys and young man.

"You too, Zane." Josh followed up Colleen's order.

Several "Yes mamam! Okay mom! Yes Sir!" where tossed over shoulders as the boys raced for the house.

Frank chuckled, "We'd best get inside before the boys inhale everything Tobias fixed."

As the group, talking and laughing, walked towards the house, another group gathered for their meal also. There was no laughter or smiles in this group. Only hardened looks, along with abusive language graced the campsite.

Two totally opposite groups if ever there was, except for one thing. One thing that would eventually draw them together. Both groups where dead set on survival.

Chapter twenty two

"Sully, how many was there?" The man that spoke had at one time been a cook at a rundown road side diner. While most considered the present to be the end of the world, Mack Jackson found it to be his homecoming.

While chaos had reined about him, he had reveled. He took what he wanted, when and where he chose. If anyone tried to stop him, they either regretted it as they lay wounded in a ditch or as most did, died regretting the fact that they should have run.

Jackson was a tall man. Rather than bulk, his body ran lean and whip-like. His long, unwashed, black hair was pulled back from his face with a leather thong, revealing a ragged scar that ran from his pointed chin up to where his right earlobe had once been, and travelled up into his hairline. The young wife that had tried to protect her wounded husband had soon rued the moment she had picked up the knife, the very knife that Jackson now wore on his belt, along with the withered ear of the woman that had sliced his off.

Although he towered above Jackson a good three inches and weighed at least fifty pounds more, Sully acted the sniveling idiot he was.

"Ah hell, must have been at least ten by my count. They was raining bullets at us like no tomorrow! If'n we hadn't pulled back when we did, they would have cut us down for sure. That's why we didn't come back with no meat. It must a been the Army, Mr. Jackson. We barely got out alive!"

Considering Sully couldn't bring his eyes up long enough to make contact with his own, Jackson figured the man was full of shit. Regardless, someone had shot at Sully and his two stupid brothers. Sully's rifle had been damaged when a bullet had slammed into the scope, and Tom had a burn across his scalp. Jackson almost wished the bullet had been one inch more to the left; it would have saved him having to waste a bullet on at least one of the brothers.

Sully, Tom and Bert had been sent out to bring back food for the camp. Jackson's men numbered close to twenty, had been twenty in fact until Sid had been shot back in that po-dunk town this last winter. Not only had they lost a man that day, but that sorry, good for nothing mule that Sid had been partial to.

Now spring was rolling in and Jackson's group of men where thinner than ever. The mule would have made a fine barbeque in Jackson's opinion. Wishing for meat didn't make it appear though, and all the men were craving protein. Men had already stripped the outlying trees of squirrel and any other varmint too slow to vacate the area.

It was still too early for the nut trees to be producing. There were plenty of greens now out in the woods, and several of the men had come back to camp with bagfuls. But Jackson had never been and would never be a vegetarian. Meat had always been the main part of his diet, even back in his childhood days when squirrel, muskrat and possum where his mainstays.

Now, Sully and his dumb-ass brothers had apparently found beef on the hoof. Honest to God steak! Instead of coming back to camp with some red meat though, they had come back sniveling about how some big, bad, bully Army men who had chased them away.

Jackson mentally shook his head in disgust as he whistled to catch the attention of the man sitting at the fire, sharpening a deadly looking Bowie knife. As the man looked over, Jackson motioned him over with a nod of his head.

Malachi Dahl was one of Jackson's prize finds. Early on, after the first chaos of the EMP, Jackson had found the other packed away in a cabin in a hollow. The man who had owned the cabin lay gutted in the front yard of the homestead. Dahl lay abed with a killer fever from the infection of the gunshot wound he had sustained when encountering the man outside.

Malachi owed his life to Jackson and they both new it. Now the giant man was Jackson's wolf, so to speak. Any clean up of an act of stupidity was always greeted with a smile. Dahl enjoyed his work enormously.

As he stood, Malachi Dahl sheathed the knife into his specially designed boot. His bald head rose above most of the men in the camp as he moved stealthily past others. The gold hoop on his left earlobe glinted as the sun's rays slipped through the tree branches above.

"Malachi, Sully here shot us some beef earlier today and managed to get chased off afore he could bring it back to us. Would you be so kind as to allow Sully and his brothers to show you where they found the cattle and possibly try and bring some back to share with our brethren?" Jackson's request was soft spoken with a slight smile.

"I think we can do that Mister Jackson. In fact, we could head out now, camp by the carcasses, keep the critters away and be back in the morning and have steak for breakfast." The soft spoken drawl didn't draw any attention to the man; only if a person was looking into Malachi's eyes would they feel death trickle down their spines.

Jackson smiled a satisfied grin, knowing full well that come morning, there would, in fact, be steak to break the men's fast. There would also be three less men to feed.

Malachi would take care of the brothers without a blink of an eye, with nary a trace to be found of them ever again. When the men were all well fed, Jackson would track down the people responsible for all this trouble. Once found, he believed he would have to teach them a lesson.

By the evening of the next day, Jackson and Dahl were hunkered down at the top of a hill, west of a farm. The sun at their backs protected them from any eyes that might just look up the ridge.

Down below, evening chores were being done by several people. Cattle lowed in a pasture behind the barn, surrounding a lone man that had brought a bucket out to the field. He was scratching the head of one cow as she shoved her head into the bucket to munch on grain.

A boy led a mule out of the barn towards another man standing in the barn yard. Once the mule was close, the man lifted the right front leg up and inspected the hoof of the animal.

"Well, lookie there. I believe I recognize that mule. I think Sid would be real happy to know that his mule will be joining him in the afterlife real soon. I still have a hankering for some mule steak." Jackson continued scanning the farm, taking in all movement as evening turned to night.

Lights appeared in windows of the house. Laughter floated up the ridge from below along with the warm inviting scents of bread and stewed beef. A shape of a man stood out vaguely, by the front gate of the farm. He appeared to be watching the road.

A rectangle of light appeared at the front of the house as a slender woman came out holding a plate of food for the guard. They spoke for a bit before she returned to the house. As she reached the porch, the man called out, loud enough for Jackson to hear,

"Tell Tobias he outdid himself again. The bread is a little piece of heaven!"

"I'll let him know! Be back out in a while with some of the peach cobbler he made this afternoon. Tis a bit more of the paradise of God!" An Irish lilt drifted upward.

"Malachi, I think an injustice has been done here. Not only are these people taking food from our mouths, stealing our transportation, they also appear to have a pretty sounding lady down there too. I don't know about you, but it's been a good long time since I ran my hand up a tender thigh of a young girl." Jackson replayed the memory of the last female company he had. It hadn't ended well for her, but he enjoyed the encounter immensely.

"Seems like maybe we should go down there and take back what's ours, Mr. Jackson." Malachi smiled as he spoke, thinking of what he was going to do to the people down below.

Chapter twenty three

One of the roosters forced a strangled crow out *twice* in a row. Rusty rolled over, grabbed Griffin's pillow and pulled it over her head. Alas, her brain already kicked into gear and thoughts began rolling into her sleep laden head. *Whose turn to get firewood for Tobias? Drew and Kate. Was there anymore cherry jam leftover from last year's supply? Probably not, it was Zane's favorite. Had she remembered to sew the hole in the toe of her sock she had laid out last night? Nope.*

Rusty groaned. If she got up right this second, she would have time to remedy the hole situation before the breakfast bell was rung. Throwing off the light blanket and sheet, she sat up onto the edge of the bed, looking over her shoulder to the other side of the mattress. Griffin had pulled night guard duty last night.

As she dressed she vaguely remembered Griffin sliding from bed at three o'clock in the morning. He had stubbed his toe on the leg of the bed as he walked around it to get to his boots.

He had sworn softly under his breath, she remembered hearing him as she had rolled over to curl up on his side of the still warm bed.

The rooster began a long, drawn out crow again but was cut off mid-squawk when a gun shot rang out in the otherwise still morning.

Rusty quickly shoved feet into socks and boots, reached for her rifle that was leaning between the bed and the nightstand and was running down the stairs when she heard another gunshot followed by a scream from Kate Blackman.

She met Josh at the base of the stairs.

"What's going on?" She started for the front window but was pulled back as Josh replied,

"Damned if I know, but Kate just dragged Drew in from outside with a gunshot wound to his head."

"Oh my God! Josh, Griffin's out there! He had the three o'clock watch. Have you seen him? I need to go find…" but Josh stopped her when he spoke.

"Come get the first aid kit, Rusty. Drew needs medical attention, Susan will be down in a few minutes. I need to check in with Kevin. He's has the east room guard duty now. I'm hoping he's seen who's out there. I need you to stay calm. Griffin knows how to disappear and stay low. I want you to stop a minute and breathe. Rushing out the door into God-knows -what is the last thing you need to be doing. Be smart, stay low and keep your weapon ready. Now go."

He had gripped her shoulder as he spoke. The touch as much as the words helped center Rusty and she ran to the surgery, grabbed the first aid kit and ran to the kitchen. There she found Kate applying pressure to the back of Drew's head with one of Tobias' dish rags. Kate and Drew both were shockingly pale.

"Kate, what happened?" Rusty opened the kit up and poured saline on a handful of gauze.

"I don't know, Rusty! We were out getting firewood and someone shot Drew! I...I don't think it's too horrible, the bullet just grazed his head, but if his had stepped back just one step...."

Kate started to sway, but Drew reached back behind himself and took hold of her hand. The touch seemed to steady both of them.

"Now Kate, let's not dwell on something that didn't happen. Why don't you let Rusty have a look- see and you help Tobias with the weapons." Drew spoke quietly, wincing at the throbbing of his head.

Tobias came out of the pantry/gun room with a rifle in each hand.

"Not sure how many of'm are out there, but I aim to keep them out of this house." Tobias went to stand by the side of the back window, scoping out the barnyard.

Morning was beginning to win the battle with night as the barnyard began to grow brighter with each minute. A chicken was out scratching by a fence post of the corral, unfazed by the rooster lying dead in front of the barn. An anxious whinny was heard from inside the barn, answered back by Borax's raspy bray.

"Hallo the house!" A man's shout came from the front of the home.

Tobias looked to Rusty, who was talking to Susan as they peered at the back of Drew's head, "Go take a peek-see out the front window. Keep yourself outta sight, girl. Take your rifle." He motioned with his chin to the rifle she had set on the table.

"Please be careful, Rusty." Susan squeezed Rusty's hand before turning her attention back to her work.

Rusty nodded, grabbed her rifle and made her way to the front of the house. As she crept down the hall to the main entry, she could hear voices from upstairs. Colleen was speaking calmly to the children as Frank made his way to the east bedroom, where Kevin and Josh currently were.

Another call came from outside, "We can talk all civil-like or not. My patience is running thin though. We'll give you bout thirty seconds, best start talking."

Rusty thought the voice was coming from the far side of the road out front of the house. As she peaked out the sidelight by the front door, she could just make out a head poking up out of the ditch across from the front gate. With the head, a rifle barrel eased up pointing toward the house.

"Civil doesn't seem to be your forte. Shooting up a man's house before the sun even pokes its head up doesn't sound real neighborly to me." Josh called out from the front second story window.

Rusty could see another man in the ditch; he seemed to be moving away from the speaker, down the ditch towards a thick stand of plum bushes. Once there, he would disappear from sight of the house.

A stair creaked behind her; she turned her head to see Colleen slowly coming down the stairs, stopping halfway to look back up at the top of the stairwell.

"Boys, stay up there. Thomas, you keep Zane and Joey out of trouble. Missy, you keep an eye on Thomas."

"Ah mom! I can take care of myself! I don't need no girl…"

"Do as your mother says Thomas, now." Frank commanded softly from further down the upstairs hall.

Frank came in sight at the top of the stairs and nodded to Colleen, "Looks to be about ten men on down the road just out of rifle range. They're all armed. If it comes to it, take down as many as you can.

Colleen came on down the stairs walking to stand next to Rusty.

"I heard," Rusty said, "Do you think any of them upstairs has seen Griffin? What do you suppose they want?"

"Time's up! Now, you can send the women folk out and maybe we'll be a lil' bit more forgiven when we come in to take care of the little'uns. Sup' to ya'll." As the man outside finished his speech, a shot rang out on the other side of the house.

Josh shouted, "They're setting fire to the back field!"

Several shots from upstairs were answered with shots from outside. A thump on the floor above Rusty's head would have sent Rusty rushing upstairs; but she was stopped from acting as a barrage of bullets hit her side of the house. The pane of glass she had been looking out of burst inward, causing glass shards to slice her left cheek and ear. She gasped in pain but aimed the rifle out of the empty framework and fired as two men rushed the front porch.

One man dropped to the ground with a brief grunt just as the other hit the door with a bone jarring thud. The door rattled in its frame but remained firmly closed.

Rusty had backed up, after the first shot, stopping when her back hit the banister of the staircase. Blood was running into her left eye, leaving her blinded in that eye. Colleen raised her rifle as she came to stand beside Rusty.

Gunshots from behind the house were being answered by Tobias. From upstairs, Rusty heard Josh bark a command at the other men as they returned fire at the attackers.

As the doorknob began to turn, Rusty and Colleen opened fire. Bullets ripped into the wood, splintering it. As sounds of gunfire began to erupt from all sides of the house, inside and out, the door slowly swung open.

Rusty's lungs refused to work and her chest burned. She was blinking rapidly, trying to clear the blood from her eye, unable to release the rifle to wipe it. Movement to her right caused her to look at Colleen. She seemed to be talking, but there was a ringing in Rusty's ears and she couldn't understand what Colleen was saying. It seemed as if the other woman was talking from down a long tunnel.

Somewhere in the back of her mind, Rusty knew the deafness was caused from the sound of their two guns firing inside the house. Still, that didn't stop the panic the deafness caused.

Whipping her head back to center, she stepped farther to the right, along with Colleen, away from being directly inline of the opening door.

The door hit the wall with a thump as the barrel of a gun showed at the door jam. Suddenly the man leapt into the doorway, waving the pistol, trying to find a target. Colleen, beside Rusty, shot once at the man. Rusty also shot and the man slowly fell forward before ever firing his gun.

Bullets drove into the wood of the staircase. Colleen crouched and grabbed the dead man's out flung hand and tried to pull him out of the path of the door.

"Help me, he's too heavy!" She ordered as she heaved herself back to compensate for the larger man's weight.

Together they dragged the man farther into the front hallway. Once he was clear of the door, Rusty kicked it shut.

Colleen rolled the man over and felt for a pulse. Looking over to Rusty she said, "He won't cause any more harm."

An ominous quiet flowed through the house and its outer surroundings, a creaking floorboard from upstairs and nothing for a moment.

Sick with worry for Griffin, Rusty stood and quietly crept to the front parlor window. She could see two bodies in the front yard grass. Another was draped over the fence, a grisly sight set above blooming daffodils and tulips. Smoke drifted from around the side of the house, she smelled the pungent odor of burning grass.

"Rusty, help me move him up against the door. That should block it enough so we can check on everyone else." Colleen spoke quietly.

They pushed, pulled and shoved the man up against the door and wedged a high backed chair between the body and the staircase.

"That should keep anyone from getting in the door. I want to go check on the kids, why don't you see how everyone in the kitchen fared?" Colleen was heading for the second floor without waiting on Rusty's response.

"Tell Kevin I love him." Rusty called out softly as Colleen disappeared at the top of the stairs.

Rusty turned back towards the hall that led to the kitchen as she reached into her pocket for more bullets for her rifle. Before she reached the room she had finished reloading and had the rifle up and ready for any action as she stepped into the kitchen.

The smell of vinegar permeated the room and there was a steady sound of dripping coming from one of the cupboards. Tobias was cussing to high heaven as he continued to scan the barn yard.

Susan and Kate were huddled in the pantry, loading the three extra rifles and two pistols that the group owned. Kate had tears streaming down her face and Rusty instantly looked for Drew. Her eyes fell to him on the floor next to the chair he had been sitting in when she had last seen him.

"It's alright Rusty." Susan smiled, "He fainted when I started to stitch the wound. He'll be a little embarrassed maybe, but otherwise fine when he wakes up. Are *you* alright? Let me finish this and I'll take a look at that cut, Rusty."

I'm alright, I think, don't worry. Kate, are you O.K.?" Rusty replied.

"Don't mind me; sobbing like a ninny, apparently this is what I do during a gunfight at the O.K. corral." Kate's laugh turned to a sob and her hands shook, but she continued working with the ammunition and weapons without pause.

Rusty looked toward Tobias and she began to make her way, ducking down to keep from being seen from outside, to the window where he stood.

"Last crock of pickles gone. Cukes won't be ready for pickling for another month or more. Blasted shame is what it is." Tobias was still muttering angrily.

"You're alright though?" Rusty asked with a grin.

"Bettr'n those fools out there." Tobias nodded out the window to one man sprawled by the back steps and two more beside the water pump in the center of the yard.

There was a dull ache in Rusty's stomach as she scanned outside. The back field seemed to have burned itself out but smoke lay in layers across the back pasture. Cattle lowed in the farthest corner of the field, away from the burnt grass.

Josh and Kevin came rushing into the kitchen. Kevin ran up to Rusty, hugged her then pulled back to examine the cuts on her face.

"Holy crap, Rusty! You have glass sticking out of your face! Doesn't it hurt?"

Rusty laughed as tears of relief pooled in her eyes. "Well, it didn't, but now that you mention it."

Tobias looked to Josh, questions in his own eyes.

"We got the one in the field, and three more trying for the house. We've pushed them back for now. Not sure for how long. One thing for sure, these men are not military-trained. Desperate, maybe, but totally untrained. It was a bit like shooting fish in a barrel from our vantage point." It was plain that Josh had not enjoyed the encounter at all.

Kevin was still examining Rusty's face and started to pick at a piece of glass before Rusty knocked his hand away.

"Stop already! Griffin? Did you either of you see Griffin?" The dull ache in Rusty's gut was twisting into a knot that threatened to take her over.

Kevin looked down briefly, then back up to Rusty's and Tobias' faces.

"Not a hair. Griffin or Dawson."

Rusty looked confused for a moment. "What do you mean Dawson? Wasn't he in his room? Griffin was to relive him at three."

"I talked to Griff in the hall when we went to relive Frank and Dawson. I never heard Dawson come upstairs. I figured he was down on the couch, so's he could beat Zane to the jam this morning." Kevin replied.

Rusty wasn't aware of Susan leading her over to a chair. She didn't feel the glass being removed from her cheek and forehead.

All she was aware of was that Griffin was once again missing.

Chapter twenty four

Griffin and Dawson watched the camp from a clump of brush up the side of the hollow. There seemed to be only three men left from a larger group, if the number of tents were any indication.

Earlier that morning, Griffin had met Dawson at the small pond where he and Rusty still managed to spend a quiet evening when time and weather permitted.

Dawson reported that it had been a non-eventful six hours. He was just starting down the path back to the house when far in the distance there was the sound of a gunshot.

Griffin trotted up as he tried to pinpoint the direction of the shot.

"Came from the east. Could have been possum or coon hunters, but I haven't heard any dogs tonight."

There were plenty of people who lived close to the farm that hunted, wild game being the only form of meat for many, though most hunting took place during the day, unless coon or possum were on the menu. Night was the optimum time to hunt the animals, both being nocturnal. Tonight though, there was no moon, making hunting difficult. Also, without a coon dog or two, no hunter would be lucky enough to just happen upon a critter in the black of night.

"Since it's been so quiet here-you up for a little jaunt in the woods?" Dawson rubbed his chin, debating if he should go let the other men, also on night watch, know before they left.

Griffin wasn't keen on traipsing through the dark woods, but wasn't willing to send Dawson out alone.

"That shot had to have been at least a mile away, but I suppose we can go."

"We can take that old deer trail over there," Dawson pointed towards the far side of the pond. "That cuts through a lot of the underbrush for a far piece. Should put us close to a quarter a mile to the shooter by my guess."

"Let's do it." Griffin chose to ignore the butterflies that started dancing around in his stomach.

The night was pleasant by Ozark standards. It was still chilly although the chance of frost had passed a few weeks back. Both men wore layers of shirts under light coats. The woods were inky black, morning not quite ready to wake, making traversing the trail a hazard. Griffin tripped more than once, cursing Dawson's night vision.

"How do you do it, man? I can barely see my own hands and you're just cruising along like its noon!" He grumbled as he caught his foot under a root and almost face-planted himself.

A rumble of laughter came from somewhere in front of him in the darkness.

"It's my super power, dude. Ya know, like Spiderman can climb walls, Wolverine has those wicked cool claws, Superman has super human strength. I got killer night vision. Don't hate man, so not cool."

"Yeah, whatever. Just slow down." As he spoke, Griffin's face hit Dawson's granite-like back. Before he could voice his complaints, Dawson hunkered down pulling Griffin with him.

They were at the top of a hollow. The darkness was broken by a several campfires down below them. The flames of one of the fires blanked out briefly as a man walked in front of it.

As Griffin moved alongside the larger man, he whispered, "Maybe a hunting party?"

A slight shake of Dawson's head followed by, "I'm guessing not. Look over there," he nodded to the far left side of the camp.

The flickering of one of the campfires cast a dim light on what appeared to be the body of a man, sprawled in an unnatural heap.

Griffin was suddenly acutely aware of the coppery scent of blood floating up the side of the hill, carried by the steam rising from the dead man.

An argument erupted from the camp as two of the four men came face to face.

"I said I was gonna take his boots. They was rightly mine anyways. Dooley took'um from that crazy old man durin' that last raid we went on." The shorter of the two whined.

"Don't see what that has ta do with the price of cotton. I got holes in my boots, and I'm taking them." The taller man stepped closer, menacingly.

As the whiney man stepped back a step, the third man's head raised in interest. He had been sitting by the farthest fire, smoking a pipe.

"Sam was the one that gutted that ol' man. They were his boots for the taking. If'n that ol' coondog hadn't raised a fuss an' bit Sam, he would have taken them boots then. Trouble was he was busy wrestling with the dog and Dooley, there, slunk in and swiped the boots." It was said quietly, but with some authority.

Sam smirked, "Yeah."

"That may be so, Jake, but, like I said I got holes in my boots!" The tall man backed down after shooting a hateful glare at a grinning Sam.

The man by the fire stood. His hair was shorn short, unlike the long, unkempt hair of the two other men. He took the pipe from his mouth as he ambled over to them. He used the pipe to point over his shoulder.

"If all goes as expected over yonder, we should have our choosin' of boots. Those men won't be needin' shoes in Hell. Now Sam, you go over there and relieve Dooley of those boots. Then if I was you...well, I'd take ol' Sam's carcass someplace far, far away. No one's gonna miss the bastard. Then again, not sure how the rest of the camp'd feel knowing you'uns were the one that did the killing."

Sam spoke again in his whiney voice, but Dawson was hauling Griffin back the way they had come so quickly that Griffin didn't catch what was said.

Once Dawson was sure they wouldn't be heard, he broke into a walk-run. Griffin, still fighting the dark, struggled to keep up. Finally, he grabbed Dawson's shoulder, forcing the other man to turn.

"He was talking about us, wasn't he? Is the farm being attacked?"

"I'm not waiting to find out, Griff. We have about thirty minutes before it starts getting light. We need to be back at the house, raising the alarm, before that happens." At those words, Dawson turned back to the trail, breaking into a trot.

Griffin was right behind him, eyes wide to gather any light they could find. A branch caught him in the face, raising welts on his cheek. The pain did nothing but sharpen the panic that rose in Griffin.

All he could think of was Rusty, back at the farm. That and the fact that at any moment, there could be an attack and no one at the house had a clue of its coming.

Making their way back down the deer trail was non-eventful, until Griffin suddenly noticed that he could make out the terrain as he trotted past. Night had retreated, and with it so did the chance of getting back to the farm unnoticed.

Just as the two men broke out of the trees, near the pond, a gunshot shattered the morning quiet.

"That's from the house." Dawson growled even as he rolled his rifle off his shoulder where it had been hanging.

Griffin reached behind and pulled his pistol out of his holster tucked in his jeans.

Silently running down the trail to the house, the pair stopped and crawled to the top of the smallish ridge at the far side of the cattle pasture. There they were able to see smoke starting to rise on the other end of the pasture. The cattle smelled the smoke and were moving towards Griffin and Dawson, away from the threat.

Shots from the house and the road destroyed any hope that there wasn't trouble. Dawson pointed towards the front corner of the pasture where a man could be seen crouched down behind a stone corner post.

Dawson brought his rifle around, peered through the scope, "He's not ours."

As he looked, the man was jerked backwards by an imaginary string. He lay sprawled in the grass, not moving.

I'll bet money that was from the east upstairs window! Josh just took that guy out! Sounds like someone at the front of the house is fighting the road! Let's follow the tree row around from the west and lend a hand."

Dawson was back down the ridge with Griffin right behind him.

Griffin knew the time had come to face his fear, the fear of having to possibly kill again. The cold, hard knot had been riding in his gut since the fight in Thompson. Now, though, it wasn't just himself he had to protect. This time it was his home, his friends, and more importantly Rusty.

By the time they reached the west side of the house, the gunfire had ceased. Dawson reported that he could see several men running down the road headed east, when he peaked out of the tree row on the side of the road. Griffin pointed to the front of the house.

"There's two down out front. Whatever happened, ours were able to even it up. I'm headed in." Griffin ran to the side of the house and followed it back to the barn yard. Two other men lay in the yard. One face down, not moving, the other staring up at the blue sky, one hand clutching his chest, the other digging down into the damp grass.

"Watch it, Daws, that one's still alive. I'm going in, I need to see Rusty." Before Dawson could stop him, Griffin disappeared around the corner of the house.

Dawson had his rifle aimed at the man as he walked towards him. Behind him, he heard Griffin call out to the house as he hit the steps.

As Dawson walked up, he kicked a handgun away from man. He squatted down, lifted the man's hand from his chest and watched as a bright red bubble rose from the man's mouth.

"Bullet caught one of your lungs. You're dying. Once a time you might have been saved. That was before the world went to hell. Now maybe we can help you go easy..." Hearing footsteps, Dawson looked up to see Josh.

The wounded man was gripped with a violent coughing fit, spraying blood into the air. Dawson grimaced as fine drops of blood settled on the arm of his jacket.

Josh joined Dawson, squatting on the other side of the man. Reaching over to unbutton the man's shirt, he viewed the man's filthy chest. Dirt and blood mingled around a bubbling hole just to the left of center.

Rolling the man over, towards Dawson, Josh shook his head and gently let the man back down. He looked up at Dawson, "No exit wound."

An agony filled groan issued from the man, as he reached up and clutched Josh's arm.

"Help me." Several hacking coughs stopped the man.

"You have a bullet rattling around in your chest, mister. There's no helping you. I told you, you're as good as dead. Tell us what your group was after, how many are there, how well armed, and we'll make what's left of your miserable life a little easier." Dawson growled, drawing the man's gaze from Josh back to himself.

The man's eyes were growing glassy, his gurgling breath growing weaker. Dawson leaned in as the man tried to form words.

"We …we wanted the women. God help us, we wanted the women."

Dawson shook the man, "How many men? Dammit man, how many men are there?"

"Stop it. He's gone." Josh sat back on his heels and swore softly under his breath.

Dawson looked up at Josh, not understanding, then back down at the dead man.

"What did he say?" Josh asked.

Dawson stood and swore as he turned and walked a few steps away from the body, circled and came back to face Josh.

"The sick bastards want the women."

Chapter twenty five

Morning was just settling in when Kevin spied movement coming down the road east of the house. He had been out at the front gate watching for just such movement. Hightailing it up to the porch he yelled through the opened door,

"We got visitors! Can't tell who they are, but their coming from the east."

Every man, excluding Drew, had grabbed a firearm and had been at the gate when their neighbors reached the house.

"Hello the house." The cry rang out from the road.

A tall man dressed in old, denim over-alls, worn boots and a drooping felt hat, holding a gleaming Civil War era rifle spoke, "Doc, everything alright here? We'uns thought you'uns might be having a speck of trouble, or just celebrating Independence Day early maybe."

The men standing behind Josh laughed at Cecil Jenkins's humor. The tall man never broke a smile but comedy always seemed to line his conversations.

Josh walked up, hand out to grip the other's hand, "Cecil, good to see you, man. Gentlemen," He looked past Cecil to the twenty-odd armed men standing at the ready, "Come on in and we'll set you up with fresh coffee and tell you what all the ruckus was. I believe it will concern us all."

Steaming coffee mugs in hand, the men and several of the women from the farm gathered in the barnyard, listening to the events of the morning.

Dawson and Griffin gave their account of the early morning scene at the camp. Josh recounted the firefight at the house then all traipsed out to one of several sheds to look at the four bodies of men that had been killed and left by their fellow ambushers.

One man pointed to a dead man. "That sum'buck there in the red flannel is Tommy Sillin. He was a bad apple from the git-go, must have got out of prison before all this." Several men nodded their agreement to the statement.

"Maybe he brought this trouble home with himself." Another of the farmers mused.

"Has anyone had any trouble at your farms of late?" Dawson looked at the men as he spoke.

Most of the men were shaking their heads; one towards the front, looked a bit surprised.

"Mr. Williams? You've thought of something." Josh looked at the middle aged man who owned a small farm to the southeast of Fort Repose.

"Well now, I just might need to apologize to my youngest. Ya see, I hung four hams in the smoke house last fall. We had two at Christmas, well you know Samson,"

Williams looked to another man, "your family came for dinner, in fact.

Then my wife was craving salt last month, she always does when she's in a family way." A sheepishly proud smile appeared on his face.

"So, I should have one ham left. So last week, I sent Clara Mae to get it. She came back saying it was gone. I couldn't imagine that being so, but once I got down to the smoke house, sure enough, all that was left was a bit of rope hanging from the rafter. I laid into Clara Mae. I figured she had left the door opened last time she'd been down to fetch meat and coyotes or some scavenger snuck in and made a meal for themselves."

Josh nodded, "Maybe scavengers of the two legged variety. Sounds like your family may have seen the grace of God, Williams. These men don't seem the type to leave a house full of women unharmed."

Carl Williams and his wife wanted a son, so every time they had another daughter, Beth would smile at Carl and say, "Next time." At last count, there were six girls helping to work the farm, ranging in ages from seventeen to two and one on the way, apparently.

Carl paled at the thought of any of his girls being harmed. Most of the men in the group had children and wives back home. The knowledge of such a large threat in the area of those families had the men gripping their weapons tighter.

It didn't take long before Josh, Frank and Dawson were leading a party of more than twenty down the road. They were tracking the gang of men, hunting them as they would hunt a rabid cur caught slaughtering sheep. It had been agreed unanimously that this gang of men was too big a threat not only to Fort Repose, but to all the outlying farms. In this new world, terrorism would not be tolerated.

Zane and the two boys had been sent in the opposite direction to take word of the incident to the women and children that had remained at their farms. They were to gather all that was deemed necessary for an extended stay. No one was to be left alone on a farm.

By late afternoon, Zane came walking back down the road leading an army of women, teenagers and children. Each person was carrying supplies, pulling wagons or leading livestock. Zane was talking and flapping his arms as he told of the attack to a group of goggle eyed children that surrounded him as he walked.

With the influx of people, housing was assigned and set up. Mothers of babies or very young children found space in the house. The others with older children set up tents that had been brought along and some found sleeping quarters in the barn.

Even as laugher and happy chatter floated over the spring air, the remaining armed men quietly walked the perimeter of the farm. There was always the possibility that trouble could pop back into their lives, so as the children chased kittens, teens helped gather wood for cook fires and adults made the impromptu camp work, many glances up the road could be seen at any given moment. Would their men come back unharmed? If the gang of violent men, God forbid, won the upcoming fight, where did that leave the people at Fort Repose?

The kitchen was a bustling hodge podge of women, girls and Tobias. The old man was in his element. He was giving advice on proper soap making with wood ash, swapping sour dough recipes and planning early summer trips to raid bee hives for wax and honey. The wax would be made into candles while the honey would be a sugar replacement.

Once Zane and the two boys had returned with the herd of families, they had stormed the kitchen claiming starvation. The ladies and Tobias had laid out jellies, jams, biscuits and fresh baked cookies. Missy surprised her brother with a fat wedge of her first homemade apple pie, made with dried apples from last autumns' crop. Once the hunger pains had been held at bay, the boys had been sent back out to help wherever needed.

Griffin and Kevin had remained behind to help organize the large group of people. Both were kept busy for most of the morning and for several hours after lunch. Several other men had volunteered to stay back to keep the farm secure. Between the six of them they scouted the woods and road in their area, looking for any sign of the interlopers.

Drew had been left behind also, much to his dismay. Josh had insisted that, due to his head wound, Drew stay at the farm so Susan could keep an eye on him. Susan had an easy job of that, as Kate seemed to be glued to Drew's side. Between the two women, Drew was unable to move far from the sofa. He didn't want to admit he would have been a hindrance if he had gone. The throbbing of his head told him, with every beat of his heart, that the couch was a much better choice.

"How are you feeling?" Kate walked in to the sitting room and sat on the edge of the couch. She lightly touched Drew's forehead, checking for any sign of fever.

Drew gave her a rueful smile, reached up and took her hand, bringing it to his mouth and gently kissed it. "I think I should have been shot a long time ago."

"What!" Kate exclaimed, a shocked look on her face.

It's a lovely face. He thought while he stroked her palm.

Drew laughed, then winced as his head reminded him it was still there. "I just meant that having you sit here with me, well, it makes it all worthwhile."

"Drew Wilder, I'll have you know that it would have been so much easier, on both of us, if you had just kissed me! Mother Mary, men are daft as..."

Before she could finish what Drew knew would probably insult poor Borax, the mule, he pulled her down and kissed her.

"You're right, it would have been much easier; silly me." He could feel her smile even as he wrapped his arms around her and drew her closer.

As the day progressed, with no sign of men returning, the inhabitants grew more and more uneasy. Griffin poked his head into the kitchen, caught Rusty's attention as she deftly peeled potatoes for the stew, and beckoned her to come outside. Rusty hurried out after asking Missy to finish.

Griffin spoke after pulling Rusty around the corner of the house. "I should have gone with them, Rusty. Kevin and I were thinking that maybe we would wander down the road a ways, just to see if we see or hear anything."

"Griffin, I don't think that's a good idea. Not unless you're planning on inviting me along. Who else is going to watch your backs?" Rusty smiled as she spoke. She had been going stir crazy in the house. Not knowing what was going on out there was driving her bonkers.

"Rusty, you heard what those men have planned for the women; I can't let you go out there! I would never forgive myself if something happened to you." Shaking his head as he spoke brought a smile to Rusty's face. The smile wasn't pleasant, and Griffin began to doubt the wisdom of telling Rusty of the plan.

"Griffin, I know full well what those Neanderthals *think* they will do to these women. Have you actually looked at the women lately? Everyone of us have been training and practicing with firearms and knives. Believe it or not, Tobias is pretty darned wicked with a blade!

Anger brought the blood surging up her neck into her face, until she resembled a red hot kettle about to blow. "If those creepers show up again, short of actually killing us, they are going to have a hell of a fight on their hands. We aren't the women we were a few years ago, Griffin. So, if you truly think I'm going to just stand here and weep into my hanky as you go traipsing off into the sunset, well you're just an idiot."

"I told you that telling her wasn't cool." Kevin, leaning against the tree by the front of the house, laughed at the looks on their faces.

"Griffin, give it up, man. You know she'll win the argument. Rusty, stop being such a hard ass. He loves you; so do I. We just don't want you hurt…or worse."

Griffin smiled, "Go get your rifle, Rusty." Before she could move away though, he pulled her into an embrace and kissed her long and hard.

"He's right, you know. I do love you."

Rusty's face softened, the anger fading, "I love you too, ya big dope. Be right back." She raced away, laughing.

Kevin ambled over to Griffin, who looked a little dazed, "Don't you know by now that she never does anything half way?" He continued in his no-nonsense tone.

"She's scary sometimes. I really think she would kill for us, you and me. Hell, for the whole farm! She's right, at least about herself. She's changed. I think we all have really, we've had too. She didn't tell you she shot the men that attacked the farm, did she? I heard Colleen tell Frank. She said that Rusty was cool as a cucumber. Said she could tell Rusty was scared, but that didn't stop her from doing what needed to be done. Sometimes I think that she was born in the wrong era. Once she realized this was our world now, she just sort of settled into it, ya know?"

Griffin laughed ruefully, "Oh, don't I know it. She's handled this life way better than I have, truth be told. Don't let her fool you, though. She would just about sell her soul for a blow dryer and curling iron. Come on, let's get going."

Chapter twenty six

"They had to have come this way; there hasn't been any spot that showed a bunch of horses leaving the road. The weeds are tall enough, we would know." Griffin spoke as he waved his hand at the plant growth on both sides of the road.

Griffin and Rusty were walking hand in hand, following Kevin who had moved ahead on the road.

Although they were all on high alert for anything amiss, hands on their rifles that hung by straps on their shoulders, the couple was enjoying the quiet countryside. The birds were singing in the air and in the trees that bordered the road and the soft breeze shared the scents of spring.

"Yeah, the county mowers haven't been doing their jobs at all!" Rusty smiled and bumped shoulders with Griffin.

"Do you hear that? Guys, stop talking and listen." Kevin had stopped in the center of the road.

Up ahead, the blacktop disappeared into trees as it curved to the south. The trio stopped.

Above the hum of insects and birdsong came faint sounds, metal on metal, men shouting, horses and mules complaining and miraculously enough, the roar of engines.

Eyes wide, Rusty whispered, afraid if she was heard the noise would stop. "Is it?"

They rushed up to where Kevin stood in the road. Rusty gripped both Griffin's and Kevin's arms, eyes shining with potential tears. "What is it?"

Griffin scowled, "Better ask, *who* it is? Let's go find out. Careful now, once we get close to the bend up there, let's move into the woods. I want to see them before they see us."

"Lead the way Hawkeye." Kevin stepped back with a flourished bow and up swept arm.

"Smartass." Griffin muttered as he took the lead followed by the siblings vying for the space behind him.

Once in the trees they moved silently, avoiding new growth of poison ivy and staying in the shadows of older trees. The ruckus of people grew louder so that they could hear the rumble of vehicles moving along the road, occasional shouts of orders being issued and laughter from men.

Thirty minutes later, crouched in a bush of sand hill plums, the trio could only stare, mouths opened, but speechless.

Stretched out a mile up the road, coming down a large hill was a convoy of transport trucks, supply trucks, older model pick-up trucks, a couple of humvees and several hundred horses and mules of every color. On all of these modes of transport were soldiers. There seemed to be hundreds of men, all coming directly towards Fort Repose and all its inhabitants.

"Holy G.I. Joe, Batman! Would ya look at that?" Kevin exclaimed, eyes wide with apprehension. "What do you think they are doing here?"

Before Rusty could answer her brother, a man riding at the head of the army of men caught her eye. "Look! That's Josh!"

"There's Dawson, look on top of that first Hummer!" Griffin pointed as he laughed.

As a unit, the three burst out of the foliage, climbed back onto the road and jogged up the road to the mass of men and vehicles, smiling ear to ear the three shouted greetings to Josh and Dawson.

Josh had been riding along side of another man also on horseback. At the sight of the three young people running down the road like grinning fools, he raised a hand in greeting and leaned towards the other man and spoke.

"Looks like you'll meet a few from our community a little sooner than expected, General Fraser. If you'll excuse me?"

"Of course, Major Martin, I look forward to meeting your group. We will continue on into New Springs and start setting up camp. If I could borrow Weapons Specialist Montgomery for the rest of the day, I could use his intel of the town." General Fraser, a lean man with gray sideburns and mustache, leaned over his own horse's neck and shook hands with Josh.

Josh looked back at Dawson, who at that very second was laughing at something a soldier had said, "I don't think that will be a problem, General. And Sir? It's just Doctor Martin now, I retired from the Army a long time ago."

"Once a soldier, always a soldier I say. Alright Martin, go see to your people." The general reined his horse to take the curve in the road that lead towards town, as Josh continued on the straightaway.

Riding up to the trio, Josh dismounted and turned to watch the convoy as it moved past them.

'It's a damn beautiful sight, if you ask me." Josh's voice thickened with emotion.

Griffin and Rusty nodded in agreement as they watched the soldiers march past. Kevin waved and whooped exuberantly back at Dawson's own rebel yell.

"What are they doing here, Josh? Is this all over? Will we have electricity again?" Rusty spoke calmly, ignoring the excited butterflies fluttering in her stomach.

Griffin smiled as Rusty spoke, knowing hot running water was at the top of Rusty's fantasies, and electricity would definitely bring, that along with too many conveniences to count.

"I'm going with Dawson!" Kevin streaked off, yelling at the top of his lungs before Rusty could say "Boo."

Even as she started to chase after her brother, Josh laid a solid hand on her shoulder.

"Let him go, I think he's safe enough with seven hundred soldiers by his side."

Griffin whistled, "Seven hundred? Where did they come from? I hope they brought their own supplies, there's no way this area can support that many more stomachs."

"No worries about that. Those transport trucks hold enough food, seeds for crops and medicine to more than take care of this area plus some. Rusty, they have been moving this way up from the Gulf. They've orders from D.C. to bring support to the middle of the country. They have been running lines back and forth from Biloxi and Gulfport. Apparently there is a large fleet of older ships and boats that the EMP didn't affect. They have been moving supplies from Florida and the East Coast. Europe has been sending supplies over since the first month this all started. Apparently, North and South America were hit by a massive solar flare. It wasn't a terrorist attack, not that certain fractions in the Middle East haven't been thrilled at the outcome. "

One of the transport trucks chose that moment to let loose two massive backfires. Josh's horse showed its opinion of the sudden noise by crow hopping, causing Josh to spend the next few minutes getting the animal calmed down.

"What? That was over two years ago! Why is help just now getting out here?" Griffin demanded.

"Easy, Griff. They had to get through that first winter supplying the East Coast with fuel and food. Remember, cities can't harvest crops and the major cities have thousands upon thousands of people. People who rely on vehicles to bring them everything they need for survival. The first spring, supplies started coming west, it's been a slow march, but they're here now.

"As for electricity, the plan is for it to make its way here by next winter, keep your fingers crossed Rusty and you should be showering with hot water before Christmas."

"Praise God!" Rusty began her happy dance, amusing the two men.

"I'm not sure what you both find so funny. As soon as we have hot water, *all* the men are scrubbing first!" Rusty laughed as she spoke.

"Gladly!" Josh countered. Griffin smiled and nodded, in full agreement with both statements.

"What were you three doing out here in the first place? I distinctly remember telling everyone at the house to stay safe and keep eyes opened at all times." Josh spoke as if he had not retired from the Army years ago, but was still in command.

Griffin had the good grace to blush, "Well, we did part of that. Eyes are wide open. Come on Josh, we waited for hours and hadn't heard anything. It was driving us nuts. So what happened? Did you find that gang?"

"It was Griffin and Kevin's idea. If I hadn't demanded that they take me too, who knows what kind of trouble they would be in now!" Rusty blurted, sounding sixteen rather than twenty seven.

Chuckling as he spoke, "Alright children, you're here now." Josh smiled as he motioned to the still passing line of military.

"They must have seen this before we did. We followed their tracks for a good five miles then they all scattered to the winds. No way to track them at that point. They must have sent a rider out before them, to scout for more victims is my guess. I'm going to step out on the ledge and guess we won't be having any trouble with that group as long as the military is showing its face in the vicinity."

"General Fraser is under orders to remain until next spring, when communication lines and some power lines should be up and running. Fingers crossed, we should be back to normal completely in three years. That's if everything goes as scheduled. Let's get back to the farm and spread the good news. I invited the general over to Fort Repose for dinner tomorrow. If Tobias doesn't have enough time to prepare he'll have my hide."

Rusty turned as Josh turned his horse, leading it down the road towards home. "That is so great, Josh! I'll cross all my fingers if it helps. Personally, I will be thrilled at not having to use an outhouse on a cold winter day."

Griffin laughed, "Rusty, did you forget that there is no indoor plumbing at the farm? It's outhouse or nothing, babe."

Rusty slid her arm to link with Griffin's, smiling as they walked.

"Maybe I was thinking about moving out of the upstairs apartment to a small house in town. You know there are lots of empty houses with perfectly good bathrooms. You know, bathrooms that are *in* the house."

Griffin walked along side Rusty, gazing out ahead of their little group. Excitement began to build as he imagined the upcoming months of change in their lives. Thoughts of something other than simple survival ran through his mind. The past years had been just that.

They had been so lucky, he realized that now. He, Rusty and Kevin had survived because of who they had been with. The group had built a safe stronghold by working together. Up until the past few days, life at the farm had been a daily struggle, at times life threatening. Now life was going to slowly slide back to what was. Back to being able to flip a switch and the room was bright. Back to those hot showers Rusty dreamt of so badly. Most importantly, back to food and medicine being more available out here in the middle of America. Yes, life was about to change, again. This time, things were looking up.

"Hey, where'd you go?" Rusty's question nudged into Griffin's musings.

He smiled and gave a low laugh, "I was thinking that since I have to bathe first, maybe I'll be kind enough to share the shower stall with you." He body nudged Rusty, pushing her away then drawing her back to his side.

"Maybe we can find a house in town with sit down benches in the shower, so that..."

"PDA. Way too much. Just saying." Josh called back over his shoulder as he continued ahead of the couple.

Rusty laughed. She kissed Griffin exuberantly before whispering in his ear, "I'll just bet we can find something to your liking."

At that, she pulled away and threw her head back, whooping to the sky. Running a few steps, she laughed happily and yelled, "I'm going to sit in a hot tub for hours! Then I'm going to microwave popcorn and sit and watch T.V. for hours!"

Josh grinned as he walked. *Life was certainly going to change. Maybe,* he thought on, *Susan would be interested in town living also. Surely there had to be at least two houses in town with large showers.*

Chapter twenty seven

About one mile from the farm the group was met by Missy Wilder. She yelled as soon as she caught sight of them, waving her arms as she ran up to meet them. Her face was streaked with tears as she tried speaking, had to stop and draw breath into her lungs before she could get words out.

"They have Susan and Kate! They said that if we let them take the women, no one else would get hurt! Daddy's in the house, Josh! They hurt him, and…" At this, Missy burst into pent-up tears.

Josh grasped the young girl by the shoulders, shaking her gently.

"Missy, who has the women? What's going on at the house?" He spoke calmly even as his gut clenched.

Rusty nudged Josh away and hugged the young girl. "Missy, who has them? How many of them? Come on, honey. We can't help if we don't know."

Missy wiped the tears away, took a breath and began, "All I know for sure is that I was sitting with Daddy…" She took a short jerky breath and continued.

"Then there was a gunshot in the kitchen. Kate screamed, then Daddy was telling me to get out the front door and to get help. I started out the door but I saw Daddy was going towards the kitchen. So, I decided he might need help.

"I snuck up the stairs and went to my bedroom. I can see part of the kitchen from there." She paused, looking at Rusty under her lashes.

"I know I shouldn't, but I always get sent out of the kitchen whenever the adults discuss something important. I'm practically a grown up now, Rusty!"

Rusty smiled and tucked some stray hair back behind Missy's ear. "Yes you are, Missy. As soon as we get this all fixed, you will be officially a grown woman. Now, what did you see?"

"Beside my bed, there's a patch of wall that was cut out at one time. Anyway, if you take out the board that was put in the hole, you're looking down the back stairwell. You can see part of the kitchen by the pantry door.

"I only saw one man; he had Susan by the arm and had a knife to her chest."

Josh swore under his breath before he could catch himself.

"Another man was talking, and I think he must have had Kate. I'm not sure, but she was crying. That man was telling the one I could see to "be careful with the merchandise," then he was yelling out the window that no one else would get hurt if they were allowed to leave with the women. Daddy must have heard what was said; because he came bursting through the kitchen door from the hall and I think he tried to shoot one of the men. A gun went off anyway. Then…"

A soft sob escaped Missy, but she took another breath and continued.

"Then there was some scuffling, like they were fighting. Kate screamed my dad's name, and then I heard someone fall and groan. I got so scared then. I'm sorry, maybe I should have stayed to listen some more, but I couldn't. I slipped back down the front stairs and out the front door. I found Colleen. She sent me to try and find you guys."

"No, you did the right thing, Missy. You were very brave. Now, we need to get back to the farm." Josh barked orders to the five farmers.

"Samson, we'll cut across the fields to come in from the back pasture. That will put us coming up to the house from behind the barn and we shouldn't be seen. We don't know that it's only two men, so all of us need to move cautiously. We can't risk our families' health.

"Tom I want you to take my horse. Ride back down and find the general. Tell him everything we know. Bring them back with you, Tom." Josh pushed the reins into the hands of the younger man.

Tom nodded and quickly mounted the horse, turning it before he was fully seated and had the horse at a full gallop before his right foot had found its stirrup.

Before the dust along the road had settled, Josh, Griffin, Rusty, Missy and the remaining four neighbors were crossing into the field next to the road. From there, they would be able to reach the farm, with zero visibility from the house.

Coming up on the farm from the orchard, the group could see that the farm's inhabitants had all moved to the back of the barn, away from the danger in the house.

Josh and the others wove through the orchard, keeping out of sight of the home. Once they reached the side of the barn, Josh caught Colleen's attention among the women.

Colleen quickly informed the group there seemed to be only the two men and that they were quickly becoming impatient and noise from in the house led Colleen to believe that Susan and Kate were not planning on going easy.

Kate was heard yelling, "Filthy gobshites!" at the men. This then led to Kate being knocked about, while Susan continued to struggle and curse the man holding her.

"Josh, Tobias is in there too, but we haven't heard a sound from him." Colleen spoke softly, but Missy heard the voiced concern and gasped.

Rusty, at her side, said "What, Missy?"

"I'm sorry, I was so worried about Daddy, I forgot to tell you. I could just make out a shoe on the floor. I didn't put it all together at the time, but Susan was looking towards that spot when I saw her."

Josh nodded, "That gunshot you heard, it could have been them getting Tobias out of the way when they entered the kitchen."

"Mom. Psst! Mom, up here!" A loud whisper came from above the group's heads. Looking up they saw Thomas Payne's head sticking out of the hayloft.

"Tommy! What are you doing up there? Get down this instant." Colleen issued the order without raising her voice.

"But Mom, we can see the men! Me and Joey and Zane, we can see the men. There's a little spot up here that we've been spying on them from. They can't see us from the window, but we can see them. Mom, Tobias is on the floor, so is Drew." Tommy's voice broke at the last. "Momma...there's blood." Tommy's voice broke at the last.

Josh, listening to the conversation, spoke. "Boys, get that ladder over by that last apple tree. We need to see what's going on." He directed two farmers.

The men brought the ladder over and leaned it up against the back wall of the barn, under the loft door.

Josh started up the ladder.

Griffin placed a hand on the ladder before turning to Rusty.

"I'll let you know what we see."

Rusty calmly rolled her eyes as she spoke, "Really?"

She then placed her own hand on the ladder; a rung higher than Griffin's and scampered up the steps.

Colleen was smiling as she too moved up the ladder. Griffin, looking a little dazed, followed after.

When Griffin climbed into the loft, the three other adults were being lead over to the front wall of the barn by the boys.

This was the prime nesting spot of the striped momma cat that the boys had laid claim to.

"We watch Tobias from here all the time." Joey announced as he pointed out the rectangular patch of light above a box of rags.

The hole in the barn wall had once been where a wench and pulley had hung out of the upstairs loft, providing the farmer a way to bring large bales to the hayloft. Once up, the hay bales would be swung over to the door. The boys had used the pulley system once, pulling each other up and down the height of the barn, before all the women of the house put a halt to the fun, insisting that the pulley system be dismantled.

"Why do you watch Tobias?"Rusty wanted to know.

She sidled up to the hole and peeked out. Sure enough, she could see right into the kitchen window above the counter by the sink.

Zane, smiling as he spoke, said, "Tobias always puts cookies in that spot to cool. We always know when he has a batch ready. We want to get down there before Kevin. Kevin's a Cookie Monster." Zane snickered.

Rusty laughed, thinking of the new name she had found for her brother.

"'Cept, Tobias is hurt now. Maybe he won't make any more cookies. You can see him on the floor." True concern rose from Zane as he pointed down towards the kitchen window.

Rusty verified, "I see him. He's lying by the pantry door. I can just see his head and shoulders. He looks like he's out cold."

"Could be he's playing possum, waiting for his chance. I don't think we can count on that happening though." Josh spoke after looking down into the kitchen himself.

Standing and looking at Rusty, he spoke again. "We need to take those boys out. They aren't going to just back off. Someone'll end up dead."

"Colleen, who's a better sharp shooter, you or Rusty?" Knowing the answer already, he waited for Colleen's response.

Colleen gave him a faint smile and simply nodded her head at the other woman.

Rusty's eyes widened, understanding what was being asked of her. Instead of denying it, calm settled over her. Four lives, lives of her friends, depended on her. She knew what was being asked; Josh didn't need to spell it out.

"Well, let's get to it, huh?" Her lips thinned as they compressed against each other. Color drained from her face, but, strangely, she felt strong and steady.

Colleen quietly took her turn at the small window and peered down at the scene in the kitchen.

The tall, bald man still stood with Susan pressed against himself, a deadly looking knife ready to impale her heart. Susan was deathly white except for two red patches on either cheekbone. That she was scared and angry was obvious.

The other man, tall in his own right, grinned as he said something to Kate, goading her into hissing a string of vulgar acts that she would inflict on the man given a chance.

The man grinned as he turned his rifle from Kate downward at the motionless form sprawled in the doorway.

Kate gasped as she reached for Drew. Before she had moved far, the man had the rifle back up in her face. Reaching out quick as a snake, he grabbed a handful of Kate's long, red hair.

"You've a smart mouth on you, girly. We'll see how your tune changes after what I do to you tonight. " He violently pulled Kate to him and savagely kissed her, grinding his lips against hers, then shoved her away.

Kate fell back, catching herself on the kitchen island. Her hand trembled as it came up to her bloodied lips. There was no fear in her eyes, though.

Colleen almost felt sorry for the man. The hate in Kate's eyes was palpable.

She stood and looked at Josh, then Rusty, "Take out the one holding Susan first. Watch out for Kate when you go for the other one, she's gonna be all over him, given the chance."

Quietly, Josh spoke to Rusty as Colleen herded the boys and Zane back down the ladder.

"Don't think, just breathe and do it."

Griffin, quiet until now, brought over a wooden box, and set it down under the spy hole. Standing up he looked at Rusty and smiled.

"Love you Babe. You got this."

Rusty's eyes met his for a second then she closed them and reached up and kissed him. "Yeah. Yeah, I do." She whispered.

Settling down on the seat, she chambered a bullet and raised the rifle. Sighting dead center of the bald man's forehead, she slowly blew her breath out, and eased the trigger back.

Chapter twenty eight

"Looks like you have it under control, Captain. Your man seemed to think you were in need of assistance." General Fraser shook hands with Josh as they walked to the road in front of the farm, where a company of soldiers loaded back into several vehicles.

"We appreciate you coming so quickly, Sir. Not knowing what was waiting for us here at Fort Repose, I may have jumped the gun a bit. Seems I forgot just how reliable my people are when the time comes." Josh paused, rubbing his hand over his cropped hair before speaking again,

"General, I'd wager a month's pension that I have the best squad in the area to take care of any insurgents that are fool enough to show their face. Although, I'd also wager that same money that my people have had enough. They just want what most want. We all want our old lives back."

The general watched his men gather and begin to head back down the road towards town, then turned back to look at the farmstead.

Already, families were heading back to their own farms. The road was crowded with soldiers, farmers and beasts as men began the short journey back to their own homes.

The farmstead was itself in the process of returning to normal.

A day had passed since Rusty had first looked down into the kitchen through her rifle scope.

In that instant, as Rusty had ended Malachi Dahl's streak of violence, Kate Blackman had moved.

When Mack Jackson's wolf had fallen, he had been stunned. That was his last mistake. Kate, seeing her chance, had scrambled for a knife lying on the wood island that she had been near.

Jackson had stood frozen at the sight of the other man falling backward, a small red dot on his forehead that Jackson failed to recognize.

Kate, in a silent stealthy movement, came up behind the stunned man. With the violence of a mother bear, she had plunged the knife into his lower back.

Jackson had a moment of mind-boggling pain as the knife blade invaded his kidney and severed the renal artery. He didn't have time for anything else as the world dimmed. Blackness swallowed him and he never felt his body slam into the floor.

The instant that Dahl's hands had dropped from her body, Susan had rushed to Tobias.

When the two men had simply sauntered into the house via the kitchen door, Jackson had fired a handgun at Tobias. The old man hadn't had time to register that the two men were not from the farm, nor neighbors.

The small .22 bullet, the last in the small handgun that Jackson had stolen, had grazed Tobias' head, doing little actual damage. It had been the terrifyingly hard crack on the counter as he fell that Susan would continue to relive in dreams for years to come, that had done more damage.

Tobias remained unconscious, now twelve hours later. Josh couldn't say for sure if the old man would ever awaken. Without modern medical tools, such as an MRI machine, Josh couldn't begin to guess what damage the older man had sustained to the brain.

Susan refused to leave the old man's bedside. Sitting in the old rocking chair, that Tobias himself favored, she watched her friend's chest continue to rise and fall. Praying for a miracle.

Kate was once again guarding Drew on the sofa. Josh had stitched Drew's head where the butt of Jackson's rifle had knocked him out. A doozy of a headache had him growling and short with her. Kate simply smiled and placed her hand on his chest to keep right him where she wanted him.

Rusty paused on her way down the staircase, watching Drew's family gather around and pamper him. Missy was once again regaling her father with the step-by-step tale of her trek on the hideously long road to find Josh and the rest of the group. At the rate she was going, Rusty figured she would have an actual marathon run before the young lady finished her tale.

Rusty continued down the stairs, pausing to smile at the group as they greeted her, and walked on out the front door of the house. From the front porch, she could see Josh and the general speaking by the gate. Soldiers were everywhere. Some loading vehicles back up with weapons that hadn't been needed when they had arrived at the farm, others helping get neighbors' belongings and children gathered as the families began the short trips back to their own farms. They reminded her of ants, all moving with a unified goal in mind.

She left the porch, waving at Josh as she headed out towards the back pasture. Everyone she passed spoke or waved to her. By now the story of the rescue in the kitchen had reached all ears. She and Kate would be known as hero's in the retelling of the events for years to come.

Zane and the boys watched her pass. The boys perched on the fence rail one on each side of Borax's head, Zane standing in front of the mule, a handful of hay gobbled greedily by the spoiled creature.

She heard them talking in hushed voices of how they wished they had seen her take out that huge man. She frowned as she walked on down the path towards the back pond.

A hero was not what she considered herself, nor did she want others to think of her as such. Three years ago, if she had heard the stories going around the farm she would have thought someone was retelling a movie they had gone to over the weekend.

Her life was so different now. Once, the life of her big cats in the zoo had filled her world. She had gone out with her friends. She had laughed and been so carefree, oblivious to her future life. Her biggest concern had been whether she would order Chinese or Italian for dinner.

As she neared the pond, she spied Griffin sitting on their log. He turned as she approached and stood.

He was more lean and rugged than he had been before. His muscles were from chopping wood and working the plow behind the horses, not from the gym. The head of brown, shaggy hair that used to be stylish in an outdoorsy way, was now wilder, pulled back and tied with a strip of leather.

Rusty wondered if Griffin knew that he had changed also. He was adapting slower than she, but he too was evolving to survive in this new world.

"Hey you." She murmured as she settled into his chest and arms that he wrapped around her.

Standing in contented silence watching the pond life form ripples on the water's surface, she wondered what this *life after the end* had in store for them now.

As if reading her mind Griffin said, "I think things are going to be alright now. This, I mean." He nodded his head, indicating their surroundings.

"I don't think *normal* is the word I would use, but, *better*? Ya know what I mean?" He murmured, his breath warming her scalp.

"I know. I think I could use some *better* right now. I don't want to keep changing. I don't like how I'm changing."

Griffin remained silent for some time, and then he spoke. His voice was thick with emotion, "You make me so proud. You've done what needed to be done. You didn't stop and think, "Would I do this three years ago?", you just did it. You've become something I'm still searching for. Don't regret what you are becoming. You're gonna survive this new thing that we have. I hope I can keep up with you."

A silent sob wracked Rusty's body and he hugged her tighter.

"You are still just as good as you were that first day I saw you. Do you remember? You were in the tiger enclosure with Rajah. He was sick and dying, but you sat there, with his ginormous head in your lap, singing some Bon Jovi song. You were a mess, tears, runny, red nose, the whole sobby deal. You were beautiful. You were brave. You were amazing. You still are."

"*I'll Be There For You*, that's the song I was singing. Rajah loved it when I sang to him. He would get that raspy purr of his going, and plop down on top of me. His purr would rumble through my whole body." Salty wetness touched her lips as she recalled the memory with a melancholy smile.

"See, you have a good heart. That's not going to change." Griffin lifted her head with his finger on her chin. Gently kissing her nose, he smiled.

The pounding of feet down the dirt path interrupted the couple's moment. Joey and Tommy, followed by a slower Zane, popped up over the rise. The second they saw Rusty and Griffin they commenced to screaming.

"He's awake! Tobias is awake! He said he'd make us cookies as soon as Susan lets him up outta bed!!"

Rusty whooped and hugged Zane when he came panting up to the group.

"That's great news, guys!" Griffin high fived both the younger boys.

"Come on! Lets go back and see if he'll make peanut butter, not oatmeal. I don't like oatmeal so much." Zane pulled at Rusty's hand, intending to lead the way back to the farm house.

She looked back at Griffin, a goofy grin plastered across her face. Just before Zane pulled her out of view, she laughed happily and called back, "Hurry! It's gonna be alright!'

Griffin and the boys began walking back. The boys pushing and shoving each other good-naturedly as they wondered aloud if Josh would let them go into town and help the soldiers.

Griff? Griff, are ya listening? Joey asked ya something." Tommy tugged Griffin's sleeve.

"What? Oh, sorry, Joey; what'd you say, bud?" Griffin pulled himself back to the present, the memory of homemade cookies filling the house with mouth water aroma fading.

I said that there's one of those church bosses with the soldiers." Joey repeated.

"Church bosses?" Griffin's eyebrows scrunched together in confusion.

Tommy heehawed in childish delight, "He means a pastor!"

Griffin laughed too, although still confused, "I don't get it, Joey. Why are you telling me about a pastor?"

Joey looked at Tommy, rolled his eyes and whispered in his friend's ear, "Grown ups aren't as smart as they tell us they are, are they?"

Tommy laughed, then seeing Griffin now scowling, covered his mouth so that only brown eyes and freckles showed.

"Joey, why are you telling me that there is a pastor with the soldiers?" Griffin was still clueless.

"Well duh, Griffin! Ya gotta have a *pastor*...," At this he glanced at Tommy, "if ya wanna get married!"

Griffin stopped in his tracks. His heart skipped a beat, his face flushed as the words sunk in.

Married? Wow! I can marry Rusty!

Joey and Tommy were outright laughing at Griffin now. His mouth hung opened and his eyes were empty looking, reminding them both of the cats when they rolled in the catnip in the herb garden.

Griffin floated back to reality, seeing the boys making fun of him and coughed and scowled, trying in vain to look serious.

"Come on boys; let's get back to the house. I'm sure the goats need milked or something."

He turned away from the boys and began walking down the path. The boys ran past him, racing each other in childish delight.

A slow smile spread across his face as a thought ran through his head.

I'm gonna marry Rusty.